THE HYBRID

BOOK FOUR IN THE ZOMBIE UPRISING SERIES

M.A. ROBBINS

Copyright © 2018 by M.A. Robbins

All rights reserved.

No part of this book may be reproduced in any form or by any electronic or mechanical means, including information storage and retrieval systems, without written permission from the author, except for the use of brief quotations in a book review.

To zombie readers everywhere. Some people may think we're weird, but they'll eat their words when the zombies are making hors d'oeuvres out of their intestines.

1

The C130 came to a stop, the tail door opened, and the ramp lowered.

Jen stepped onto the ramp and took a deep breath. She coughed and wheezed in another breath. "Holy shit, what's the humidity here?"

Mark walked past her with his arms spread. "Good old Southern air. Humidity's probably around ninety percent."

Zeke bounded down the ramp in his black ninja costume. *He's got to be burning up.*

"Need to get off the ramp," the crew chief said. "We've got to get going."

Jen scanned the airport. Commercial aircraft from small Beechcraft to national airline 747s were parked, dark and silent. No baggage handlers or their tractors. No guys waving planes to or from gates. The place was dead. "Where are we supposed to go?"

The crew chief adjusted his headset and shrugged. "No idea. Our orders were to drop you off at Hartsfield-Jackson airport and we've completed our mission. Now, move back, please."

Howell jogged down the ramp and to a stairway underneath a gate. "Can't change their orders, so let's see what we've got."

Jen adjusted the double-bladed axe on her belt and followed Howell and Zeke up the stairs. Mark stayed close behind her, scanning the area. None of the schedule boards were lit and all the snack and news outlets were shuttered.

"Reminds me of a Stephen King novel," Zeke said. "Had a scene that described this perfectly."

"And where was everyone in that one?" Mark asked.

Zeke smiled. "I don't do spoilers."

"I say we head for the baggage area," Jen said.

A sound echoed from farther down the terminal hallway. Jen lifted the axe from her belt, while Howell and Zeke pulled their pistols and Mark's mace appeared in his hands.

"Isn't that the direction of the baggage area?" Zeke asked.

"Screw it." Jen wiped sweat from her forehead with the back of her hand and strode across the shiny tiles of the terminal. "I want to get to the CDC, give them my blood, then reload and go after Butler."

Mark hurried to keep up with her. "How are you going to find one zombie in the middle of millions of them?"

"Don't know. Don't care." Jen sniffed. "All I know is I won't find him by sitting on my ass here."

Two men in black suits appeared from around a corner fifty yards away. Jen stopped and reared back with the axe from pure instinct. The suited men reached into their suit jackets but froze when Howell and Zeke aimed at them.

"Who are you?" Howell asked.

One of them removed his hand from his jacket and raised it, displaying a badge. "Homeland Security. If you're the survivors from Fairchild, then we're here to take you to CDC Headquarters."

Jen relaxed and lowered the axe. "I hope you're taking us there in something with air conditioning."

Zeke and Howell lowered their weapons. One of the Homeland Security men, a blond with windswept hair who gave off a surfer vibe, stepped forward. "Agent Daniels." He nodded toward the other agent, a thirty-something man with dark features and piercing brown eyes. "Agent Rodriguez."

Rodriguez flashed his badge. "Pleasure. We've got transportation out front. We were going to pick you up at the drop-off point, but all entry to the flight line is blocked."

Mark slid his mace into his belt. "Let's get the show on the road."

Daniels led the way through the concourse and to baggage claim. Outside, a black limousine with government plates was parked at the curb. Rodriguez opened the back door.

Jen climbed in and nearly passed out. "It's like an oven in here."

Rodriguez climbed into the driver's seat and started the vehicle. Seconds later cold air blasted into Jen's face. "Ahh."

Zeke sat next to her, while Howell and Mark took the seat across from them. Daniels jumped into the passenger seat and the limo took off.

Jen leaned back, enjoying the arctic air flowing over her face. *I don't remember ever being this hot in my life.*

Howell peered out the windshield. They were just leaving the airport.

"Not much traffic," he said.

Daniels shifted in his seat and turned to the passengers. "You'll get a full debriefing I'm sure, but we have a fuel crisis. With several refineries down and others in danger from the horde, all commercial aircraft have been grounded and gasoline is being rationed."

Mark frowned. "Any attacks since Fairchild?"

"Smaller towns," Rodriguez said. "Nothing big. But the military is pouring into the front line bases like Mountain Home Air Force Base in Idaho and Nellis Air Force Base in Nevada."

They came to a stoplight, and Rodriguez slowed as the light turned red. Several cars passed through, each one loaded with people. A cop car went the other way. Jen caught a glimpse of a cop in the passenger side in full riot gear. *Smart idea. Makes it harder for the zombies to bite through.*

The light changed and Rodriguez turned onto Norman Berry Drive. They passed a strip mall with a smattering of cars and trucks in the parking lot. Two cabbies stood outside their parked cabs, talking.

Goosebumps formed on Jen's arms. "You can turn the AC down a little. Even an Alaskan girl has her limits."

Daniels adjusted the fan speed as the limo entered an intersection. A pickup flashed by mere feet in front of them and Rodriguez slammed on the brakes, spilling Jen onto the floor. Tires squealed, followed by a sickening crunch.

Doors opened as Jen pulled herself up. A late-model truck, its front end pushed in, rested against the folded side of a minivan. Jen hopped out of the limo and joined the others running to the crash site.

The truck's driver's door popped open. A thin, middle-age man in worn jeans and a straw cowboy hat stepped out and collapsed to his knees.

"You OK?" Jen dashed to his side.

He shook his head as though to clear it. "Just a little dizzy."

She put a hand on his back. "Why don't you sit down.

I'm sure an ambulance is on its way." She eased him to the ground.

She stuck her head in the truck. An older woman sat on the passenger seat, her head lying against her window, a star pattern radiating from the impact point of her head. Jen checked her pulse. *Weak and fluttering.*

"What you got?" Mark's voice came from behind her.

She backed up and straightened, cracking her neck. "This lady needs an ambulance sooner rather than later." She nodded at the man in the straw hat. "He's shaken up, but should be OK."

Daniels jogged over. "Ambulance and backup on the way. Three minutes out."

"Backup?" Jen asked.

Rodriguez joined them. "New protocols. Everyone needs to get back to the limo."

"But there are people hurt over here," Zeke called out. He stood next to the ruined minivan, his face pinched. "There are eight people crammed in here."

Howell leaned over the minivan's driver, a thirtyish brunette with a gash on her forehead that bled like a stream. "Some of these people will die if they don't get help now."

Two other vehicles stopped on the side of the road and four men came running. "Need any help?"

"No." Daniels waved them away. "Everyone away from the vehicles, Now."

Howell gestured to the others. "Come on. Orders are orders." He herded them to the limo.

One of the civilians, a bear of a man with a shock of red hair, unbuckled the old lady from the truck and gently lifted her. "I'm not leaving someone's grandmama to die." He bent down to lay her next to the Straw Hat Man, and she wrapped her arms around his neck.

"Bless your heart," the redheaded man said. "Strong enough to hang on."

The old lady clenched his neck and pulled him closer. "What the hell?" He struggled to keep his balance before letting out a scream and pummeling the woman with his fists.

She fell back, a chunk of bloody flesh in her mouth. The redhead stumbled away, holding onto his gushing wound.

The old lady swallowed her prize whole and fell upon Straw Hat Man, who struggled against her.

Yelling came from the minivan. Two of the other men raced back to their vehicle and peeled out. A pair of legs stuck out of the driver's door and kicked in the air as a desperate scream came from inside.

Jen pulled her axe and sprinted for Grandma Zombie. She'd just torn Straw Hat Man's soft abdomen open and had her face pressed into his guts like a kid bobbing for apples at a Halloween party. Jen drove her axe blade deep into the back of Grandma's head and she went limp.

Shots came from the limo. Zeke leaned across its hood and aimed at the minivan, smoke coming from the end of his barrel. The thirtyish woman lay facedown by the minivan, the back of her head blown out.

Zeke and Mark ran to the van. Mark cracked the skull of a teenage boy as he leapt from the vehicle, and Zeke shot through a window several times.

A growl made Jen spin. Straw Hat Man's yellow eyes locked on her. Her axe still buried in the old lady's head, she backpedaled out of the zombie's grasp. Another shot came from behind and a bullet hole appeared in the zombie's eye. He collapsed in a heap.

Sirens approached, and Jen wiped blood from around her eyes. *Some of these freaking things splatter like a bitch.*

She jerked the axe from grandma's skull and wiped it off on the old lady's dress before slipping it back into her belt.

An ambulance screamed to a stop, its siren cutting off. Two police cars stopped behind it and four cops in riot gear and weapons jumped out. Jen stumbled toward them. "You guys can relax. We took care of it for you."

A cop with a shotgun aimed it at her. "Let's clean this up, men."

Three other rifles swung her way.

2

Jen froze. *The hell?*

Zeke aimed his pistol at the cop with the shotgun. "Anyone shoots and you get it first. In the face."

The other cops swung their rifles toward Zeke. Howell aimed at them.

"You're outnumbered," a young black cop said. "Might as well drop it."

Daniels and Rodriguez pulled their handguns. "Homeland Security," Daniels said. "The safety of these people is a national security priority."

One of the cops looked at the one with the shotgun. "What do we do, Sarge?"

The sergeant kept the shotgun pointed at Jen. "If you're Homeland Security, then you know the protocol and why we need to follow it."

Mark had his hands up and his mace in his belt. "What protocol is the one where you pull guns on us?"

"Anyone in contact with the reanimated dead has to be put down," the sergeant said. "Anyone who is terminally ill will be put down." He glanced at Mark. "A bullet to the head."

"I thought everything was supposed to be OK back here," Jen said. Mark flashed a frown. *Now he's not so sure his family is safe.*

"Things are under control," Daniels said. "But it comes at a price. That's why every ambulance has a police backup."

"But what if you're shooting uninfected people?" Zeke said. "Ever think about that?" He blinked, and for the first time Jen noticed the dark bags under his eyes. She'd slept on the plane and assumed the others had, too. *Did Zeke stay awake to watch over me?*

"Sorry, kid," the sergeant said. "Can't take the chance."

Jen slipped her axe into her belt, the movement causing the sergeant to stiffen. She put her arms up. "I'm not gonna do anything. But let me ask you something."

The sergeant nodded.

Jen gestured to Zeke and Howell. "Put your weapons down."

Howell lowered his pistol. Zeke hesitated, but dropped his arm to his side when Jen glared at him.

"That's better." She turned her attention to the sergeant. "How long is it taking for someone infected with a bite to turn?"

He shrugged. "Couple of minutes."

She looked at her watch. "You've been here for five minutes. She pulled her lower eyelids down. "No yellow. See?"

The sergeant pursed his lips and looked at his men. One of them shrugged. "She's right, Sarge."

"What if it's a new strain?" the sergeant asked. "Could be one that takes longer."

"Strain my ass." Jen walked toward the limo. "I'm out of

here. You want to stop me, you'll have to shoot me from behind."

"Wait."

Jen halted and glanced back. The sergeant lowered the shotgun and gestured at the others to do the same. "Stand down."

Jen let out a breath she hadn't realized she'd been holding. Growling came from inside the minivan. "Looks like you have some cleaning up to do."

The sergeant nodded. "Let's go." The cops circled the minivan.

Jen puffed her cheeks and let out a breath. "Can we go now?"

Mark put an arm around her shoulder and led her to the limo. "How the hell do you keep getting away with calling a bluff?"

She gave him a quick hug. "Charmed, I guess."

Rodriguez started the limo and they all jumped in.

A cascade of gunfire came from the minivan as they pulled away.

Broken only by wisps of clouds, the blue sky looked gorgeous as long as Jen was in the air conditioning. *I hope the CDC keeps it cool.*

The limo pulled onto Interstate 85 and the amount of traffic picked up. Still, it wasn't anything like she'd heard about Atlanta's congestion.

Staring out the window at the vehicles passing by, she nudged Zeke.

"What's up?" he asked.

"Notice all these cars are full? You don't see any with just the driver."

The faux leather seat squeaked as Daniels turned around. "Not only has rationing been ordered, but it's against protocol to have fewer than half the capacity of a vehicle."

"Is it like this everywhere?" Mark asked. "How safe is it?"

Daniels shrugged. "These are national protocols. They're everywhere."

"How about safety?" Mark asked. "Heard anything about Birmingham?"

"Alabama?" Rodriguez asked. "Nothing specific there. There've been a few outbreaks, and only two of them became nasty. One was Dayton, Ohio. Lost a hundred and twenty people before it was brought under control."

"Another in Connecticut took a few dozen," Daniels said. "And you know what the common thread ran through both of these?"

"Let me guess," Jen said. "Protocols weren't followed."

Daniels pointed a finger at her. "Bingo."

They exited onto Route 78, passing pedestrians and bicyclists crowding the sidewalks.

Jen lay back and closed her eyes. She pulled her bloodied shirt away from her chest to get air under it, and it stuck to one side. "Freaking zombie guts. I should do a detergent commercial. 'Just a cup in the wash gets the zombie goop off.'"

She leaned back and drifted off.

JEN WOKE WITH A START, her hand going to the axe on her hip. The limo slowed as it approached a gate with a guard shack. Iron bar fencing on a brick base stood ten feet high and separated several high-rise type buildings from the street. The tallest, a concave-shaped silver building covered in windows, glinted in the sunlight.

The limo stopped next to the guard shack and

Rodriguez rolled down his window. "These people are here at Dr. Cartwright's request. They have no credentials, so I'm vouching for them."

The guard lifted a piece of paper on a clipboard and peered into the back of the limo. His gaze settled on Howell. "Name?"

"Sergeant Howell."

The guard peered at Mark. "And you?"

"Mark Colton."

The guard nodded as he consulted the clipboard. "You two. Names."

"Jen Reed."

"OK."

"Zeke."

The guard squinted. "Zeke what?"

"Zeke Tripp."

Jen laughed. "Your last name's Tripp?"

Zeke looked hurt. "Yeah. What's wrong with that?"

"Nothing," Jen said, stifling another laugh. "It's just not the name I'd come up with for someone who's so stealthy on their feet."

The guard wrote something on the clipboard. "Good to go. I'll notify Dr. Cartwright you're on your way." He stepped away from the limo and gestured to another guard, who rolled the gate open.

Rodriguez put the limo in gear and drove into the compound. He pulled up to the main doors of the concave building.

Jen followed the agents in and sighed when a blast of cold air brushed her face. "Heaven."

An older guard just inside the door waved them all by. "Dr. Cartwright is waiting for you in her office."

An elevator ride to the eighth floor took seconds, and they stepped out into a carpeted hallway with soft lighting. Jazzy instrumental music played through speakers in the ceiling.

Daniels led them twenty yards down the hallway and into a reception area. A receptionist with a headset looked up and pressed something on her desk. "They're here, Doctor." She nodded and looked at Agent Daniels. "She'll be just a minute."

Thirty seconds later a buzz and a click came from a set of double doors to the receptionist's side. "You can go in," she said.

Rodriguez held one of the doors open and ushered everyone in. A large, spacious room with floor-to-ceiling windows, Cartwright's office was filled with sunlight. Framed artwork hung on one of the walls, while another had pictures and plaques. One that caught Jen's eye showed Cartwright and the President next to each other in what looked like a serious conversation.

From what I've seen of Cartwright, everything's a serious conversation.

Cartwright sat at her desk facing them. She stood. "Jen, good to meet you." She made eye contact with each of the others in turn. "Good to meet you all."

She gestured to a comfy looking sofa and a set of chairs. "Please have a seat."

Jen took one of the chairs, while Howell took the other. Mark and Zeke plopped down on the sofa.

Cartwright took her seat. "I received the message you passed along at Grand Forks. I have to say, it left me wondering if the message wasn't misunderstood by the airman who communicated it to me. Would you mind filling me in?"

Jen leaned forward, her elbows resting on her knees. "Butler died and came back a leader."

"But a super leader," Zeke said. "Kinda like a top-level Boss on one of my video games."

Cartwright's eyes stayed on Jen. "And so it's true that he controlled a horde that numbered in the millions?"

"It's a fact, Doctor," Howell said. "Threw his hands in the air and every damn one of those things froze in place."

Cartwright rubbed her chin. "That gives me a lot to think about."

Jen fidgeted in her seat. "I'd like you to take my blood so I can go back out there and find Butler."

Mark's eyebrows rose. "I don't think that's a good idea."

Cartwright frowned. "We don't know where he is. Besides, I need you here with me. There's much to be done." She tilted her head forward and peered at Jen over the top of her glasses. "And I need you for more than your blood."

Jen stood. "All due respect, Doctor, but I was there at the beginning of this thing. I lost my Dad, Chris, Doc, and too many other people to count. I want to end it."

Cartwright sighed. "And you will. But as my assistant where you'll do more to end this catastrophe than you could by charging to your death."

Her face softened. "It may make you feel better to go after Butler, but your impact will help many more people if you stay and work with me."

Jen rubbed the heels of her palms into her eyes. *Feel like I haven't slept in days.*

She took a deep breath and let it out while puffing her cheeks. "OK, Doctor. I'll sleep on it."

Mark stood and stretched. "Come to think of it, I think we could all use a shower, some food, and a good sleep."

Cartwright pressed a button on her desk. "Amy, please send Agents Rodriguez and Daniels back in."

The two agents appeared immediately. "Take them to the hotel and get them settled," Cartwright said.

"Yes, ma'am," Rodriguez replied.

A young woman in a pant suit burst into the room like an eager intern. "Dr. Cartwright. News from the front."

"What is it?" Cartwright asked.

"There are multiple coordinated attacks against Boise, Las Vegas, and Malmstrom Air Force Base in Montana."

"How many?" Zeke asked.

"Tens of millions." The woman turned to Cartwright. "General Loomis said all three locations could fall within a day."

3

Cartwright pointed to the window-length blinds. "Close those. Let's get Colonel Rogers on video at once."

"Ma'am," the woman said, "I'm sure he's tied up with the attacks at the moment."

Cartwright stared at her. There was no anger in her face, but the woman hurried to close the blinds. Cartwright typed on her keyboard and a section of the wall behind her slid over and revealed a fifty-five-inch flat screen. The word "Connecting..." displayed on it.

An older soldier's face appeared on the screen. Silver eagles adorned the collar of a wrinkled uniform shirt. His lower eyelids drooped and his eyes had red blood vessels crossing the white sclera like a lightning strike.

"Dr. Cartwright," he said. "We're in emergency mode—"

"I want details," Cartwright snapped. "Some very important decisions may need to be made based on the situation."

The colonel's shoulders drooped. *This guy looks like shit.*

"Evacuation of Malmstrom AFB in Montana to Grand Forks AFB is in process. We estimate forty percent of the personnel and eighty percent of the equipment will make it out before the base is overrun."

"Shit," Mark breathed.

Cartwright's expression remained unchanged. "And Las Vegas?"

"It's going to fall." Rogers rubbed a knuckle in each eye. "And it'll be soon. There's a line of traffic heading east all the way to the Arizona border. Hordes have broken off and are flanking the city on the north and south. It's obvious they plan to attack the refugees and encircle the city."

Howell cleared his throat. "What about Nellis AFB?"

"Overrun an hour ago, but we evacuated all personnel and essential resources."

Zeke looked up from studying his fingernails. "What about Area 51? Did you fly the UFOs out of there?"

Jen clasped his forearm and shook her head. "Not the time."

Rogers ignored Zeke. "Boise is fifty-fifty. We've launched constant air strikes from Mountain Home AFB. It seems to have kept the horde at bay for now."

Cartwright sniffed. "Keep me updated, Colonel."

The screen went blank.

"Butler's behind it," Jen said. "I need to find him and finish what I started."

"Don't be foolish," Cartwright said.

"Excuse me?" Heat flooded Jen's face.

Mark turned toward her. "I wouldn't put it that way, but what are you going to do? Just walk through the horde looking for him?"

Zeke slapped the table. "I'm with you, Jen."

Jen sat back and let out a long breath. "I don't see me doing any good here."

"Why?" Cartwright asked. "Because you can't be out there acting like a hero?"

Jen frowned. "Wait a minute—"

"You are the only living person on Earth who received a fully concentrated inhalation of the spores," Cartwright said. "That makes you unique, and a superb test subject to find a cure."

"But we don't even know if that will help," Jen said.

"But if it does?" Cartwright asked. She raised a hand, the thumb and forefinger a half-inch apart. "We're this close to a cure. If you want to do something to stop this scourge, then help us with that."

Jen stared at the floor. *She's right. And so is Mark. How the hell would I find Butler without becoming a zombie snack? Still, I'd rather do something more than get poked with needles.*

Jen sighed. "Where do I go to donate blood?"

Cartwright gestured to the young woman. "This is Cindy Hirt. Cindy, please escort Miss Reed to the phlebotomy office and bring her back to me when she's done."

"Yes, Doctor." Cindy turned to Jen. "Miss Reed?"

Jen stood. "Lead on."

"I'll go with you." Zeke stepped to her side.

I love this guy. The little brother I never had. "I think I'll be safe in the building. Why don't you stay here? I won't be gone long."

Zeke pursed his lips and nodded.

She followed Cindy into the hallway and onto the elevator, where the assistant put a key in the panel and turned it, then punched the lowest button. Lower Level Four.

The elevator dropped quickly and quietly, stopping at their destination in seconds. The doors slid open with a slight *whoosh*, revealing a set of double doors with the words "Authorized Personnel Only" stenciled on them.

Cindy took an access card that hung from her hip and swiped it through a reader on the wall. A blip and green light from the reader and Cindy pulled the door open.

The room was thirty feet wide and almost that long. A rack of stainless steel morgue refrigerators lined part of one wall, while two stainless steel autopsy tables sat in the middle of the room, under large operating room lights hanging from the ceiling. Jen squinted. All the refrigerator doors had keyholes. *Keeping someone out or something in?*

Cindy strode through the room, pushed open a door on the other side, and walked through. Jen gave a refrigerator door handle a tug as she passed it. It didn't move.

She hurried after Cindy and into a hallway with a dozen doors, six on either side. She went to the first door and peeked into the small eye-level window. An old lady lay in a hospital bed with her eyes closed. A respirator mask fitted on her face, her chest rose and fell rhythmically.

What the hell are they doing down here?

She hurried to keep up with the assistant and followed right on her heels as she pushed through a pair of swinging double doors and into a large cavernous room. Buzzing lights hung from a high ceiling, casting a bright glow that reached into every corner of the room.

Jen stopped in her tracks. Lining both sides of the room were a dozen large cages, each with a snarling zombie inside. As if on cue, they strained at their chains as Jen and the assistant entered.

The assistant glanced over her shoulder and stopped. "They're very secure."

Jen blinked. "I'm not afraid, just surprised."

A door opened at the far end of the room. A balding middle-aged man with a blond handlebar mustache stepped out with a clipboard in his hand. "What do you have for me?" His gaze swung to Jen. "And who is this? Why is she in a restricted area?"

Jen followed Cindy to the man. His white lab coat had "O'Connor" embroidered over the pocket. "I'm Jen Reed. I'm guessing you're the vampire who's going to suck me dry."

The man looked at Cindy then back at Jen before he put his hand out. "Dr. O'Connor. I work with Dr. Cartwright."

Jen shook his hand. "Why don't we get on with this? These zombies are giving me a headache."

O'Connor looked at the zombies as if he'd just noticed they were there. "Of course. I'm so used to them, I've mentally blocked them out." He turned. "Follow me."

Jen followed him and Cindy into the room he'd appeared from. Two other people in lab coats sat at separate tables, one working on a computer and the other peering into a microscope. Shelves of vials and jars, as well as equipment like a centrifuge, lined the counters.

The door closed, cutting off the growls of the zombies.

"Please, have a seat." O'Connor gestured to a blood drawing chair. She sat as O'Connor rustled through drawers, pulling out a plastic open-ended tube with a nasty-looking needle at the end and several glass tubes with rubber at one end. Jen flipped the padded arm of the chair across her lap and rested her arm on it.

"Have you found out where the virus came from?" she asked.

O'Connor froze and glanced at her, then went back to rummaging in the drawer. "We're working on it."

He turned around and wiped down the crook of her arm with a swab. The sting of alcohol fumes made Jen crinkle her nose. "What have you found out so far?"

O'Connor stabbed her arm and Jen flinched. She looked

away. She didn't mind shots or needles as long as she didn't have to look at them stuck into her body.

Cindy had wandered over to the lab tech on the computer, and they spoke in hushed tones.

Jen looked around at the well-equipped lab. Doc would've liked it there. *Doc.* His name still brought a twinge of guilt. *I'll never forgive myself for his death.*

A sharp jab in her arm caused her to pull in a breath.

"Just another minute," O'Connor said.

Jen looked down. A full tube lay next to two more. A fourth one was in the vacutainer and filling up fast. He pulled that one out, shook it, and laid it down, before slipping another in.

Looking away, Jen said, "Looks like a lot of blood."

"You'll be fine," O'Connor said. "But I want you to sit here for ten minutes afterward just to make sure you don't feel faint."

He removed the needle and pressed a cotton ball over the wound. "Hold this here, please."

Jen pressed a finger onto it as O'Connor taped it down. "I'll pass on the ten minutes," she said. *If I haven't passed out from anything that's happened in the last month, then I won't pass out from this.*

O'Connor shrugged.

Jen eased out of the chair and straightened. "Cindy, can we get going?"

Cindy looked over from the computer, said something to the lab tech, and walked to the door. Jen joined her, and as soon as the door opened, the zombies came alive again.

They'd made it several feet from the lab when Dr. O'Connor appeared in the doorway. "Ms. Hirt, Dr. Cartwright is on the phone for you."

Cindy put out a hand. "Wait here." She hurried into the lab.

"Shit," Jen said. "And I have to stay out here and listen to this?"

The door eased shut and the zombies went silent as if someone had flipped a switch.

Jen peered at each of them. All of their eyes were on her. *What the fuck?*

She took a few steps toward the exit, and the zombies straightened like soldiers at attention, their heads swiveling to keep their gazes latched on her. Jen approached one, a young redhead, and its soulless eyes locked on hers. *Nothing. Not even a spark of life in them.*

The lab door opened and the zombies went wild, gnashing their teeth and growling at Cindy.

Well, well. If this ain't some creepy shit.

4

Jen followed Cindy back into Cartwright's office. What was going on with those zombies? Why did they quiet down when only she was there? Could it be another mutation in the virus? *Should I tell Cartwright?*

"Just in time," Cartwright said.

Jen broke from her thoughts. "Just in time for what?"

Howell stood next to Cartwright. He put his hand out. "Dr. Cartwright has assigned me to be her liaison with the Pentagon. I'm taking tonight's train to Washington."

Jen shook his hand, then pulled him into a hug. "Sorry to see you go." She broke the embrace. "You saved our asses more than once."

Howell smiled. "And you've saved a lot more with your observations and reports."

"And she'll save even more by helping us find a vaccine," Cartwright said.

Howell stopped in the doorway. "I think it'll take all of us to save humanity."

He disappeared into the hallway just as Mark and Zeke walked in.

"Where have you two been while I was getting stabbed?" Jen asked.

Zeke smacked his lips. "Got a bite to eat."

"Knowing you, it was enough to feed a bear," Jen said.

Mark laughed. "Don't you know it."

Cartwright's phone rang and she put on a headset. After listening for a few seconds, she said, "Yes. Bring them up."

Mark and Jen exchanged puzzled glances. Zeke examined a spot on the rug and scuffed it with his foot.

A knock came from the door a few minutes later. "Enter," Cartwright said.

An older woman with gray streaks in her curly black hair walked in with a younger version of herself. The younger woman's eyes grew big and a smile broke across her face as she yelled, "Mark." She raced to Mark and threw herself into his arms.

"Michelle," Mark said, his voice muffled as he held her close. He loosened his grip on her and put an arm out toward the older woman. "Mama."

The older woman shuffled to him, her eyes glistening, and buried herself in his arms.

Jen watched the reunion, half-fascinated at the emotional display and half-jealous there would be no such experience waiting for her. She glanced away, a little embarrassed about her feelings.

Cartwright sat behind her desk, her face neutral. *Is she really like that, or does she have to practice that look?*

Mark looked up. "Thank you, Dr. Cartwright. It's so good to know they're safe, and now I can escort them back to Biloxi."

"About that," Cartwright said, "I have an offer for you."

Mark frowned. "What offer? I'm not leaving them alone again."

Cartwright adjusted her glasses. "Precisely. I'd like you to become CDC Headquarters' Chief of Physical Security."

"But wouldn't I have to stay here for that?"

Cartwright nodded. "Yes. But part of the offer is that your mother and sister can stay here free of charge. Room, board, security. And that security will be provided by you."

Mark's mouth dropped open. He looked at his mother. "What do you think, Mama?"

Michelle nodded. "Take it. Things are getting weird out there. I know we'll be safer here with you."

"OK," Mark said. "I'll take it."

"Excellent," Cartwright said. "You can go through inprocessing tomorrow." She pressed a button on the phone. "Please come in."

The door opened and Cindy appeared. "Take our new Chief of Physical Security and his family to their quarters, and show them where to eat."

Cindy ushered the family through the door. Mark stopped and looked back at Jen. "I'll introduce you and Zeke later. I really want them to meet you."

Jen waved him on. "Looking forward to it. Just enjoy the time with your family." Her thoughts went unbidden to her mother and father.

Cartwright clasped her hands and laid her elbows on her desk. "Miss Reed and Mr. Tripp."

Jen turned to her. "So what've you got in your black bag for us?"

Cartwright frowned. "Bag?"

"Sorry," Jen said. "Wizard of Oz reference."

Cartwright sniffed and her phone buzzed. She pressed her earphone and listened. "Very well. Send him in."

What next?

The door opened and a man stepped in. He looked a couple years older than Jen and wore a pair of snug jeans and a T-shirt that showed every muscle. While not a bodybuilder, he either worked out or had a physical job.

Jen's pulse picked up. *I hope this one's for me.*

Zeke yelled, "Wayne." He rushed the man, who caught his skinny frame in a crushing hug.

"Zeke, I've been worried about you. I thought you died when they nuked Anchorage."

Zeke released Wayne and gestured to Jen. "Jen and Mark saved me."

Wayne's gaze fell on Jen and she swallowed. *Hazel eyes.*

"Uh," she said, "Zeke saved us more than once, too."

Wayne's eyebrows rose and he looked at Zeke. "Really? How?"

"I had this great katana." Zeke mimicked slashing the air with a sword. "It wasn't real, but it was close enough. It broke on a zombie."

Wayne glanced at Jen and she nodded. "He's amazing with a katana."

"Then we'll have to find you a new one," Wayne said. "We're heading back to Rhode Island tomorrow."

Zeke froze. "But I can't go back. I have to watch over Jen." He turned to her. "What would she do without me?"

Wayne glanced at her and winked. "She can come with us."

Jen's face grew hot. *Is he coming on to me?*

"Impossible," Cartwright said. "Jen must remain here."

"Then I have to stay," Zeke said. "Sorry."

Wayne sighed. "I couldn't get you to leave Anchorage a few years back when I did, so I'm not surprised I can't get you to join me now."

The door opened and Cindy stumbled in carrying two wooden boxes, one about four feet long and the other half that. She placed the boxes heavily on the table, arranged them side-by-side, and left without a word.

"What's that?" Zeke asked.

Cartwright approached the table. "I'm offering the two of you positions in Homeland Security."

"I'm not into groping passengers at the airport," Jen said.

Wayne snickered, catching Jen by surprise. *A sense of humor, too. Take me now.*

Cartwright's face hardened more than usual, if that were possible. "Homeland Security, not TSA. You'll both work for me—Jen on the cure and virus mutations, and Zeke as protection for Jen."

Zeke hovered by the table. "But the boxes. What's in them?"

Jen caught Wayne's eye. "He must've been a riot at Christmas."

"You have no idea."

"The boxes," Cartwright said, "are part of your equipment. You'll receive firearms, a badge, and these."

"A badge?" Zeke said. "Do we get a car with a siren and lights?"

Cartwright's pushing too hard. "And what do the badges get us other than a discount at the donut shop?" Jen asked.

"You'll be federal agents. They'll get you access and assistance from pretty much any agency."

Zeke's eyes shined. "Come on, Jen. Sounds fun to me."

Jen frowned. *I'm getting boxed in.* "Will it get me military assistance when I go after Butler?"

Cartwright ignored her and pointed to the long box. "That's yours, Mr. Tripp."

Zeke pulled the box toward him and lifted it, testing its weight. "What can it be?"

He flipped three latches on it and tilted the top back. An audible gasp escaped his mouth. "Oh. My. God."

Zeke reached in and lifted a deadly, beautiful katana. "Stainless steel, thirty-six-inch blade." He stepped back from the others and gave it a practice swing. "The balance is perfect. I could take out a ton of zombies with this." His eyes met Jen's. "And this one won't break."

Cartwright's face wore the glimmer of a smile. She had Zeke. *And she knows that's one way to get to me.*

Jen pointed at the remaining box as Zeke removed a scabbard from his. "I suppose this is for me."

Cartwright nodded.

Jen opened the box and reached in, pulling out a tactical tomahawk. *Like the one Griffin had in Point Wallace.*

"The blade is eight inches and the length with the handle is almost eighteen," Cartwright said. "Doc told me you admired this weapon that someone had in Point Wallace."

Jen hefted it. "Damn this is light and balanced well." The sinister blade looked like it would cut through bone, and the sharpened steel point on the other end would no doubt pierce skulls.

She removed a sheath from the box looped her belt through it before inserting the tomahawk. "I suppose this is mine only if I stay."

Cartwright leaned against her desk and crossed her arms. "I understand why you want to go after Butler, and you could do that, but you would be dooming many people."

"Not if I kill him."

"Killing him won't stop the virus," Cartwright said.

"We've got to stop the dead from coming back. Emergency protocols have been put in place, but they aren't enough."

"We heard about the protocols on the way here," Jen said. "I'm not surprised that killing people who may not be infected doesn't work well."

Cartwright took her seat. "There are more than that. Armed personnel are stationed at all hospitals to make sure the recently deceased don't reanimate EMTs go out armed. All pet mammals have been quarantined."

Jen lowered her eyebrows. "Just the mammals?"

Cartwright nodded. "We've determined that the virus only infects mammals. But even with the quarantine, there are plenty of strays and other wildlife that die of natural causes, then reanimate and infect others."

She clasped her hands together and leaned forward, her elbows resting on the desk. "The truth is we're just barely staying ahead of it. There have already been multiple outbreaks that could have spread out of control. With the military and national guard committed to the threat in the west, we rely on federal, state, and local law enforcement agencies, and it isn't enough. Local militias have been formed to help fill the gap."

Jen swallowed. *Two threats, Butler and the virus, and I can't battle them both at once.*

"OK," Jen said. "I'll stay and help with the vaccine." She walked to the door. "But once it's ready, I'm out of here and on Butler's ass. And I expect your help in getting to him." *And in the meantime I'm going to find out what's going on with those whacked-out zombies downstairs.*

5

The next morning Jen and Zeke strolled out of the administrative office. A shower, a good night's sleep, and fresh clothes had done Jen wonders. She stopped in the lobby and pulled her access card out. "I wonder how much of this place we can get into?"

Zeke scratched the shaved side of his head. No longer in a ninja costume, he wore a T-shirt with sleeves he'd carefully ripped off, and a pair of black cargo pants. Somewhere he'd found gel and had turned the hair on the unshaven side of his head into a series of spikes. "We should be able to go anywhere." He pulled his Homeland Security Agent badge from his pocket. "Bad boys. Whatcha gonna do?"

"Put that thing away, Dirty Harry. I don't think it's going to do much for you while we're here." She smiled. "But once we're on the road again, we'll travel like a boss."

Zeke shrugged and dropped the badge back into his pocket. "So what are we going to do? I'm already bored." He adjusted the katana scabbard on his back.

Jen strode to the elevators. "Cartwright's supposed to be

in some meeting for the next few hours, so let me take you on a tour of the basement."

Zeke followed her into the car. "That doesn't sound very exciting."

Jen punched the bottom button. "It's right up your alley."

"Why?"

"They've got zombies down there."

Zeke's face lit up like a Christmas tree. "Can I kill some?"

When they arrived on the lowest level, Jen made a beeline to the card reader by the door. *Let's see how much Cartwright trusts me.*

She slid her card through the reader and the door answered with a buzz and a clunk. She pulled it open and stepped into the hallway.

It looked the same as it had the night before. Buzzing lights hung overhead, glinting off the tile floor. Not a speck of dust lurked in the corners, and the air held a slight tinge of ammonia.

"What's this?" Zeke asked.

Jen peeked in the first door's window. A young man lay in a bed with an IV in his arm. His sunken eyes stared at Jen. "Not sure. I don't know if they're treating them here, or using them to test the vaccine. I'm guessing they're guinea pigs."

She led Zeke to the windowless swinging doors that led to the zombies and pushed one open.

The zombies went into a frenzy, straining at their chains as soon as Zeke and Jen entered the room. Zeke reached back and gripped his katana's handle, ready to pull it into action.

Looks like they're only quiet when one of us is out here.

She strode to the lab door and pointed at Zeke. "Wait out here for a minute."

Zeke shrugged and leaned up against the wall with his arms folded.

Jen pushed the door open and eased it shut behind her. She didn't even need to press her ear to the door to know the zombies were still going apeshit. *Guess that disproves that theory.*

"Miss Reed," Dr. O'Connor's voice came from behind her. She spun. He sat on a stool, loading a syringe with an off-color liquid. "You're just in time."

Jen pulled the door open and waved Zeke in, then gestured to O'Connor as Zeke entered. "Dr. O'Connor. Doctor, this is Zeke."

O'Connor nodded at Zeke, then turned to a thirty-something lab tech with Clark Kent glasses. "Randy."

The lab tech looked up. "Yes, Doctor."

"You're with me on this one."

Randy wiped his hands on his lab coat. "Yes, sir."

O'Connor swept past Jen and Zeke and paused as he opened the door. "You'll want to see this, Miss Reed."

He led them to one of the cages. Inside, on a gurney, lay the older woman Jen had seen in one of the rooms the day before. *Why do they have her in a cage now?*

Randy removed the padlock from the cage door and held it open as O'Connor stepped inside. An IV drip ran into the woman's arm and a mask covered her mouth and nose while a machine on a wheeled table next to her made wheezing sounds.

O'Connor waved Jen in. The zombies raised their din to another level. O'Connor leaned toward Jen and Zeke. "Mrs. Jawolski volunteered to be a test subject for the vaccine. In return, her family is living in a government-secured location."

"What's wrong with her?" Zeke asked.

"COPD," O'Connor said. "She's at the end. That ventilator is the only reason she's still alive." He inserted the needle into a rubber stopper halfway up the IV line and pushed the plunger until the contents were emptied. "Randy?"

Randy looked at his watch. "Injection at 8:41 a.m."

Jen watched the old lady's face. Was she supposed to turn? To die?

O'Connor herded them out of the cage. "Now, we wait. Ten minutes." He strode into the lab.

Randy locked the cage door and followed the doctor.

"This science stuff is pretty lame," Zeke said. "I expected something more interesting."

Jen gave him a playful slap on the back. "Now that I think about it, damn near every time you say you're bored, it suddenly gets un-boring and we're up to our necks in zombie shit. How about wishing for something else for once?"

Zeke sighed. "I've got to take a leak."

Jen pointed to the lab. "Saw an open door in the back of the lab with a toilet."

"Be right back." Zeke disappeared into the lab.

The door closed behind him, and the zombie racket cut off. *Shit. So it wasn't my imagination last time.*

Jen walked up and down the rows of cages. Every zombie stood quiet and followed her with their eyes.

She stopped at one, a fresh-looking woman with a pinched face and wide shoulders. She reminded Jen of her sixth grade teacher, Mrs. Curling.

Jen stood right up to the bars and stared into the yellow eyes. No hunger. No hate. Just blank.

The zombie's eyes flickered and startled Jen. "What the hell was that?"

The lab door opened, and Mrs. Curling flung herself at the cage door. Jen tripped and landed on her ass.

Zeke stood in the doorway, laughing. He rushed over. "Sorry." He chuckled again and wiped tears from his eyes as he pulled her to her feet. "After all we've been through, I never expected you to get freaked out by a zombie in a cage."

Jen put a hand to her chest. Her heart felt like it was going to explode through her ribs. She took deep breaths until it calmed.

Zeke stopped laughing and put an arm around her. "Are you OK? I didn't mean to laugh."

Jen managed a smile. "Why not? I would've laughed at you."

He chuckled. "It was funny."

"Miss Reed." Dr. O'Connor and Randy stood at the old lady's cage. "Time to complete the experiment."

Randy unlocked the door, and O'Connor examined the old lady. "Blood pressure and heart rate unchanged. EEG shows decreased brain activity."

"What does that mean?" Jen asked.

"We believe the more active the virus becomes, the more it stimulates the brain," Randy said. "It's a good sign that the activity is down in the test subject."

"Significant," O'Connor agreed. "This is the first vaccine to achieve it."

He removed the IV from the old lady's arm. "Everyone leave the cell, please."

Jen stepped outside the cage with Zeke. Randy held the door open.

O'Connor turned off the ventilator and removed the old lady's mask. "Life support removed at 8:53 a.m." He rushed from the cage and Randy slammed it shut, securing it with the lock.

The ECG showed a continued heartbeat. The old lady's chest rose, and a startling gasp came from her lips. Her eyes opened, showing only the whites, and the old lady took a huge wheezy breath, then went still. The ECG flatlined.

"Time of death," O'Connor said. "8:55 a.m."

"How long before she turns?" Jen asked.

Randy kept his eyes on his watch. "Between forty and sixty seconds."

"Twenty seconds," Randy said. "Thirty...forty...fifty...sixty."

Jen watched the old lady. She hadn't moved.

"Seventy...eighty...ninety."

O'Connor licked his lips. "I think we may have done it."

"One hundred...one hundred ten...one hundred eleven."

"Randy, unlock the door."

Randy looked up from his watch. "Are you sure? Shouldn't we wait a little longer?"

O'Connor held out his hand. "Nonsense. The poor woman's been dead for more than twice the time of any other reanimation. Give me the key."

Randy handed O'Connor the key, and the doctor removed the lock. Jen and Zeke exchanged a glance. Zeke already had his hand on the hilt of the katana.

Jen slipped her tomahawk from its sheath. "Not sure that's a good idea."

O'Connor bent over the woman with a stethoscope in his ears, listening to her chest. "Remove the monitoring equipment from her."

Randy hurried to the other side of the bed and removed the blood pressure cuff from the old lady's arm.

O'Connor straightened with a smile. "I do believe we've done it."

The old lady's yellow eyes shot open and fixed on O'Connor.

6

The zombie rolled off the table and landed cat-like on the floor. Jen grabbed O'Connor by the collar and yanked him behind her.

Randy turned to run but the zombie sprung onto his back, knocking him to the floor. Jen shoved O'Connor at Zeke and reared the tomahawk over her head. She brought it in a wide overhead arc and drilled the point into the old lady's skull. The zombie slumped and Jen pulled her off Randy.

Randy's lab coat was torn and bloodied. *Is that his blood or the zombie's?*

He scrambled to his feet, breathing harshly, and bent over with a hand on his back.

"Are you bit?" Jen yelled.

He shook his head. "I've got a bad back and the test subject just made it worse, but I'll be OK."

"Jen!" Zeke held O'Connor on his feet outside of the cage. The doctor's head sagged.

Jen pointed the tomahawk at Randy. "Stay where you are."

"What do you mean? I just told you I'm OK."

Jen backed out of the cage, shut the door, and locked it. "No time to argue. If you still have those baby blues in a half hour, then I'll let you out."

"Let me the hell out of here now." The lab tech rattled the cage door.

Jen sheathed the tomahawk and put an arm around O'Connor. "Let's get him in his lab."

The caged zombies continued with their racket. *That shit's getting old. I'm with Zeke. We should drop them.*

"Wait." Randy stood at the cage door. "He's got a heart condition. There are pills in his bottom right-hand desk drawer. Keys are in his pocket."

Zeke held the lab door open while Jen walked O'Connor inside and lowered him to the floor. O'Connor's complexion had gone pale and his breathing shallow. "Call for help," she said.

Zeke closed the lab door then picked up a phone and pressed a button. Seconds later, he said, "Emergency in Dr. O'Connor's lab. He doesn't look well." He paused. "Right."

Jen rummaged through O'Connor's pockets and pulled out a ring of keys. She rushed to the desk and tried one. It didn't turn. "Dammit."

The next key she tried didn't fit. She glanced at O'Connor. Zeke hovered over him. "Is he still breathing?" she asked.

Zeke's eyebrows knitted. "Barely."

Jen picked a small worn key and shoved it into the lock. She turned it and jerked the drawer open. Hanging files took up most of the drawer, but a small prescription bottle lay in the front. She snatched it up and ran back to O'Connor. Zeke had folded up a lab coat and placed it underneath his head.

Jen opened the bottle and shook out two pills. "Need water."

Zeke dashed to a water cooler and returned seconds later with a cup.

"Hold his head up," Jen said. She placed the two pills in O'Connor's mouth and tipped the cup to his lips. "Come on, Doctor. This'll make you feel a lot better."

The lab door burst open and two emergency medical technicians rushed in. Jen backed away next to Zeke.

The EMTs took O'Connor's vitals, then placed him on a wheeled gurney and rolled him out the door, the growls of the caged zombies filtering into the lab.

Jen sank into the chair at O'Connor's desk and leaned back. "Guess that vaccine didn't work."

Zeke poured himself a cup of water. "But it delayed the change. Maybe O'Connor's on the right track."

Jen grunted in agreement. *How much time do they have to get it right?*

She opened the drawer she'd found the pills in and replaced them. A name on a file folder tab caught her attention and she pulled it up. In scrawling handwriting, the tab had "Dr. Jeffrey Morgan, Project Svengali" written on it. She pried the folder open. It contained a half-inch-thick stack of papers. The first was a progress report from Morgan on CDC letterhead. *What the hell? That asshole actually worked here? Why didn't Cartwright tell me?*

The lab door opened and Rodriguez and Daniels strode in. "Dr. Cartwright wants to see you."

Jen eased the drawer closed with her foot and pocketed O'Connor's keys. She pushed past the agents and out the door. *Were the human experiments Morgan was charged with performed here as part of Project Svengali?*

Zeke nudged her and pointed to Randy's cage. The lab

tech stood at the cage door watching them with his arms folded. "Think I can get out now?"

Jen strode up to the cage and looked him in the eye. "No yellow. Looks like you're clean."

Zeke opened the door and Randy stepped out. "How's Dr. O'Connor?"

Jen shrugged. "We gave him the pills and the EMTs took him away. They didn't tell us squat."

Randy ran a hand through his hair. "I came here to work with Dr. O'Connor. He's had these attacks a few times before, and each one seems to be worse."

He thrust out his hand to Jen. "Thanks for being so quick to help him out."

Jen shook his hand. "He'll be OK."

"I hope so." Randy shook hands with Zeke, then trudged toward the lab, stopping at the door.

"I owe you one," he said and disappeared into the lab.

CARTWRIGHT STOOD BEHIND HER DESK, staring out the window when Jen walked in. The doctor broke her trance and sat, then waved Rodriguez and Daniels away. "Dr. O'Connor is stable for now. Please tell me what happened."

"He gave the old lady the vaccine, waited ten minutes, then pulled the plug," Jen said. "She died and didn't come back within two minutes, so Dr. O'Connor assumed she wasn't coming back at all."

Zeke sat on the couch. "Dr. O'Connor went in to check her out and she popped up like a jack-in-the-box. Jen pushed the doctor through the cell door to me and took care of the zombie. Dr. O'Connor's face had paled and he couldn't stand on his own."

"We got him in the lab and gave him his pills," Jen said. "Before we knew it, the EMTs were there."

Cartwright steepled her fingers. "Two minutes? We're getting closer." She slammed a fist on her desk. "But not close enough." She leaned back in her chair and rubbed her eyes with the heels of her hands. "We're running out of time."

"It's not that bad, is it?" Jen asked.

"When the outbreak started in Alaska, we had time to rally the troops in most of the rest of the states," Cartwright said. "Thanks to you and Doc, we had information up front on how the zombies behaved and how best to kill them. And on top of that, we had troops deployed to most larger cities to avoid major outbreaks."

Cartwright sighed. "But with all the federal and National Guard troops now on the front lines, we're entrusting local law enforcement and civilian militias. Training videos on how to spot and suppress outbreaks and how to fight the zombies are playing constantly on TV stations, cable stations, and the internet. Despite this, more and more incidents are occurring. I fear we're on borrowed time."

Zeke moved closer to Cartwright's desk, a definite gleam in his eyes. "Sounds like we should get out there and kick some zombie ass."

Cartwright shook her head. "Not a chance. I need Jen here until we have a vaccine."

"I'm betting the mammals are causing the outbreaks," Jen said.

"Quite probable," Cartwright said.

Zeke cracked his neck. "We've seen zombie dogs."

"And a moose," Jen added.

Zeke's mouth dropped open. "Really? I would've loved to have seen that."

Cartwright plopped her open hand on the desk, a ring on her middle finger making a loud noise. Jen and Zeke looked at her.

"We've quarantined all pets," Cartwright said. "But how many squirrels die in a day? Skunks? Beavers?"

Shit. "It only takes one," Jen said.

"Exactly," Cartwright said. "That's why perfecting the serum is so critical. Dr. O'Connor believes that once he perfects it, he can make it deliverable by spraying from the air. That'll immunize the wildlife as well as humans. The military will send back aircraft to undertake that mission when we're ready."

Agent Rodriguez hurried into the room.

"What is it?" Cartwright asked.

Rodriguez glanced at Jen and Zeke. "That task you gave me this morning. I have an update."

Cartwright stood. "Would you two excuse us, please? I'll let you know if there's any news."

Jen led Zeke into the reception area. Rodriguez closed the door behind them.

Cindy walked in. Her pantsuit looked like it had been ironed only moments before. "Is there anything I can help you with?"

"We're good," Jen said as she continued into the hallway.

Zeke followed her onto the elevator. "Where are we going?"

"Outside," she said. "I need some air. Starting to get claustrophobic in here."

Jen pressed the "L" button, and the elevator doors slid closed.

I need to tell Zeke what I found out about Morgan, but not here. Once we're away from the buildings and any interruptions.

The elevator slowed and stopped. The floor indicator showed they were at the fifth floor.

The doors opened and a crowd of screaming CDC employees pressed inside.

"What the hell?" Jen yelled.

A woman with wild eyes shrank against the elevator wall. "Hurry! Close the doors before the zombies get in."

7

The crowd pinned Jen to the wall of the elevator. "Out of my way," she screamed.

She squirmed and pushed off the wall, but didn't go anywhere. "Zeke, we need to get out."

"Over here," he yelled. He'd been trapped in a corner by the panicked mass. Even as skinny as he was, he wasn't able to squeeze out.

He raised an arm above his head. Jen notice the gun in his hand just before he pulled the trigger. The discharge was explosive in the tight confines of the elevator and the babbling group of employees was stunned into a momentary silence.

"Get off this fucking elevator and let us out or we start shooting," Jen bellowed.

The employees blocking the entrance piled out, and Jen muscled a man in a cheap suit aside. She broke into the corridor, where a swell of humanity pressed back into the elevator as it complained with an earsplitting buzz.

The doors closed on three people still trying to get inside. Jen pulled a younger man back. "There isn't room."

He swung his fist at her face and she ducked. His momentum threw him into a tech, who pushed him off.

Zeke pulled the other two people from the elevator doorway and the doors slid shut.

"Now look what you did," a gray-haired woman with thick glasses shouted. Tears streamed down her face.

Jen pulled her pistol and raised it into the air. Zeke followed suit. The crowd quieted.

"Homeland Security Agents," Jen said. Zeke pulled his badge and raised it next to his gun. He had an odd grin on his face and his eyes gleamed.

Little shit's having a ball.

Jen lowered the gun. "I want two answers and I want them fast. Which way are the zombies and how many of them are there?"

A woman in a nurse's uniform pointed down the hall. "Medical wing. I saw at least eight, but there are a lot of people missing. They may have been bitten."

Jen removed the tomahawk from its holster. "I suggest the rest of you find the damn stairs instead of waiting around here. Now, out of our way."

The crowd parted and Jen and Zeke hurried down the hallway. When Jen glanced back, everyone had disappeared. *Good. Fewer people we have to worry about becoming zombies.*

The tactical tomahawk was much lighter than the axe she'd previously had, but she'd seen Griffin tear zombies apart with his. *I'll just have to get used to it fast.*

She stopped at the end of the hall and Zeke peered around the corner, his katana ready to strike. "Nothing."

Jen stepped into the corridor. A nurses' station stood empty, but an overturned cart of food and paper scattered across the tile floor told her the zombies had been through.

Blood streaks decorated the walls like some gruesome avant-garde art.

A dripping sound came from the station. Slow and heavy. *Drip. Drip. Drip.*

Jen motioned Zeke to take the far wall and she huddled against the near one. She took a step and listened.

Another step and waited.

She and Zeke were in tune. As much as they'd faced together the previous few weeks, they'd learned each other's tendencies and had become a dangerous team.

Zeke motioned to the right. Jen nodded. They reached the station. Corridors went off in four directions from the nurses' station. A set of double doors was closed on one, but the others were propped open.

The constant dripping grated on Jen's nerves. Jen stepped behind the counter and stopped. Blood pooled around a half-eaten heart on a shelf. It ran down the side until it ran out of shelving and dripped steadily on an upturned bedpan. Jen took a towel lying on the floor and tossed it over the bedpan. The dripping continued, but much quieter.

"Which way?" Zeke asked.

Jen considered the corridors. No use going into the closed one. *But which of the other three? Wish I knew the layout.*

Something flashed down the corridor on her left. Her peripheral vision picked it up, but it had disappeared by the time her eyes had snapped that way. Zeke looked in that direction, too.

"As good a choice as any." Jen entered the corridor. Zeke took the opposite side of the hallway and together they made their way down the hall. The doors they passed were solid, with no windows, and all closed. Jen opened the first one she came to. Baskets of laundry crowded the room, but there were no signs of anything, living or dead.

A clattering came from an intersection ahead. Something metallic hit the floor and spun, making a racket. Jen put a finger to her lips and motioned Zeke to move ahead with her.

She reached the intersection and scanned both ways down the corridor. A pan, like the type used to hold surgical instruments, lay on the floor several feet away.

"We're getting too deep in here," Jen said. "If there were zombies down here, they should've attacked by now."

O'Connor stepped into view at the next intersection. His glasses gone and his mouth stained red, he glared at Jen.

"So that's how this shit started." Jen sprinted toward him and O'Connor darted out of sight.

"Wait for me," Zeke yelled.

Double doors on Jen's right burst open as she passed them, and two dozen zombies spilled into the hallway between her and Zeke, who skidded to a halt and took a defensive position.

Five of the zombies turned toward Jen. She gave the tomahawk a hefty swing at the first one, but its light weight threw off her timing and the blade zipped inches from the creature's face.

Shit. She pulled her pistol and dropped the zombie with a shot to the forehead.

More zombies flowed from other doors. "Zeke. Run!"

Jen took off the other way down the hall and around a corner. She had ten yards of corridor before it became a dead end. "Are you shitting me?"

The last door on the left stood open. Jen sprinted through it, slammed the door shut, and locked the large deadbolt.

Zombie fists pounded on it, but the thick wood barely shuddered. *I'll be safe in here.*

She turned to survey the room and her mouth went dry. O'Connor stood in a corner several feet away, his yellow gaze fixed on her. Jen aimed the handgun at O'Connor's nose.

"Sorry, Doctor. Consider this your termination notice."

O'Connor continued to stare. *Like the zombies downstairs.*

Jen lowered the gun just enough for a better view of the undead doctor. She stepped to the right and O'Connor's eyes followed her. She moved to the left and he never broke eye contact.

"What the hell's going on?" she asked.

O'Connor tilted his head back like he was going to let loose with a screech, but he swallowed, his Adam's apple bobbing. He lowered his chin and reconnected his gaze with Jen.

A drop of sweat rolled down her cheek. *This is something new. Are they evolving again?*

O'Connor's mouth opened, then closed. *Damn thing looks like it's trying to talk.*

Entranced, Jen lowered the pistol to her side. "What are you trying to say?"

The doctor's jaw worked up and down. He looked like a fish out of water struggling for a breath.

"Jiinn."

The blood rushed from Jen's face. *Did he just say...*

O'Connor shook his head like a dog with a toy. He glared at her. "Jin."

You're telling me these fucking things are going to start talking now?

"Are you saying my name? Jen?"

O'Connor's head jerked forward, then back.

Jen gasped. "What the hell?"

Muffled gunshots came from the distance, getting closer. Jen took a step toward O'Connor. "Dr. O'Connor, is that you?"

O'Connor's head jerked to one side, and then to the other.

Jen took a deep breath. Her pulse raced and a rock settled in the pit of her stomach as an unbelievable thought rose in her mind.

It can't be.

"Butler?"

The corners of O'Connor's mouth pulled back in a grotesque leer.

8

Jen raised the pistol, her hand shaking. "I'm going to find you and enjoy killing you again, you son of a bitch."

The blast of a gun came from just outside the door.

O'Connor raised his arms in a surrender gesture.

"How are you going to surrender when you're not really here?" Jen aimed at his forehead.

"Help," O'Connor grunted.

Jen licked her lips. *How'd I get stuck talking to a dead man who's talking through a dead man?*

"Why the hell would I help you?"

O'Connor's mouth worked, but no sound came out.

The door burst open and three security officers rushed in, their handguns cocked and ready. The largest stepped in front of Jen and fired.

"Hey," she said, "I can take care of myself." She pushed the security officer to the side.

O'Connor lay flopped over a chair, the top of his skull missing.

Shit. Now I'll never find out what the hell is going on.

Jen spun. "Who asked you to do that?"

She looked up into Mark Colton's soft brown eyes.

He smiled. "You're welcome."

"Why'd you kill him?" she asked.

His brow furrowed. "What? What else do you do with a zombie?"

She bit her lip. *Shut up, Jen.* She shook her head. "Think I banged my head on the wall when you shoved me. I'm all right now."

"You should have someone look at that," Mark said.

Jen gave him a half smile. "Like I said, I'm fine. Besides, looks like the medical department's become a bit short-staffed."

A security officer with her blonde hair in a bun approached. "Chief, looks like we're clean."

"I want all security personnel not on perimeter duty to clear every room in every building on the campus. Start with this one," Mark said.

The security officer nodded and rushed out of the room, barking instructions on a radio.

Zeke jogged into the room, relief flooding his blood-specked face when his eyes met Jen's. "There you are," he said.

Jen pulled his lanky frame into a bear hug. "I don't know why zombies go after you. You wouldn't even make a quick snack."

Zeke gave her an awkward pat on the back and stepped back. "Except for worrying about you, that was a hell of a lot of fun for me and Crusher."

"Crusher?" Jen said. "As names go, it's better than Betty, but your katana slices. Wouldn't Crusher be a better name for a mace or a bat?"

"It's named after a character on TNG," Zeke said.

"TNG?"

"*Star Trek Next Generation.*" Zeke beamed. "Wesley Crusher."

Jen sighed. "If nerdism was a super power, you'd rule the world."

Mark rolled his eyes. "Let's get you two somewhere safe."

Two hours later, Jen and Zeke walked into Dr. Cartwright's reception area. Cindy looked up from her computer. "Go right in." Without waiting for an acknowledgment, she went back to work.

O'Connor's assistant, Randy, leaned forward in a chair in front of Cartwright's desk, while the doctor faced a large monitor with a split screen. On one side was Howell's somber face and on the other was a young woman about Jen's age. She wore wire-frame glasses and sported short frosted hair. Cartwright glanced over her shoulder. "Good timing. Have a seat." She gestured to the empty seats in front of her desk.

Turning back to the monitor, she said, "Sergeant, I need a transport aircraft immediately. This is a matter of the highest national security."

"That's what I told the general, ma'am, but he shot me down. There's a fierce battle in Boise and all transport aircraft are needed there."

Jen took her seat. *I hate coming in on the middle of conversations.*

"What do we need the plane for?" she asked.

The woman on the screen said, "Is this Jen?"

Cartwright nodded and pointed at the screen. "Jen, this is Dr. Preston. Donna, this is Jen Reed."

Donna offered a petite smile. "Good to meet you, Jen."

"Pleasure," Jen said. "What do we need the plane for?"

"To bring Donna here," Cartwright said. "She works in a CDC-affiliated lab in Boston and is our next best option after Dr. O'Connor."

"I thought the train ran to Boston," Zeke said. "Why can't she take that?"

Donna rolled back from the screen so her wheelchair was in view. "Before the disaster, I would've had no problem taking the train," she said. "But now that it's the sole method of mass transportation, it's filled to capacity, which makes it very difficult to navigate in my chair."

Howell looked off camera. "Be right there." He turned to the screen. "Boise is critical and there's been another major attack. This time it's Phoenix."

He disappeared from the monitor and Donna's face filled it.

"Can't Randy work on it here?" Jen asked. "He worked with O'Connor."

Randy scoffed. "That's like asking an operating room nurse to perform brain surgery."

"Clearly that's not our best option," Cartwright said. She adjusted her glasses and looked at the ceiling. "We're out of best options, and now we're down to the best of the worst."

"Donna," she said, "if we can't get you down to our lab, we'll get our lab to you."

Randy frowned. "So I'm going to Boston? Not sure that's a safe trip."

Cartwright shot him a withering glare. "Relax, we need you here in case O'Connor left any written notes that haven't been transcribed into the system. You're the only one who will know where they are."

Randy's shoulders relaxed.

"No." Cartwright stood. "I'll send the serum on the train with some agents."

"Serum?" Zeke asked.

"Dr. O'Connor had two doses of the latest iteration of his serum," Donna said. "He used one in his last experiment."

"But it didn't work," Jen said. "So why do you want it?"

"It's the result of all his research," Donna said, "and I don't want to start from scratch if I can help it."

"Fine," Cartwright said. "I'll have two agents leave on tomorrow's train with the serum."

Donna stared from the screen. "As long as one of those agents is Jen."

"What?" Jen said.

Cartwright scowled. "I need Jen here."

"And Dr. O'Connor's lab notes are adamant that a component of Jen's blood is essential for the serum," Donna said. "I don't know how much I'll need."

"So the human pincushion needs to go along with the serum." Jen leaned back in the chair. "Great." *And it'll get me farther away from Butler.*

Cartwright stared at the wall. And uncomfortable silence fell over the room.

Cartwright turned back to the monitor. "I don't like this at all, but I don't see another solution. At least, not unless the military would shake some air transport loose."

Zeke jumped to his feet. "I go where Jen goes."

Jen smiled. *My hero.*

Cartwright sighed. "We'll set it up on this end. I'll send you the specifics."

Donna nodded. "Looking forward to it. And looking forward to meeting you, Jen."

Jen waved at the camera. "Same here. How about some of that famous clam chowder when we get there?"

"You've got it." The monitor went blank.

Cartwright swiveled the chair around. "Things are getting dicey out there, even on the east coast."

"I thought the protocols were keeping things under control?" Zeke asked.

"Go ask O'Connor how well that's turning out," Jen said.

Cartwright stood. "You'll leave on tomorrow morning's train. Jen will carry the serum, and Agents Rodriguez and Daniels will accompany you."

"My brother's heading home on that train," Zeke said. "Can he travel with us?"

"I think that's a great idea," Jen interjected. Zeke and Cartwright looked at her. Cartwright's eyebrows were raised.

Jen shrugged. "Safety in numbers, right?"

"Very well. Have him report with you to the armory to be equipped for the trip. Then muster outside the front entrance of this building by 6:00 a.m."

Zeke smiled. "Back into action."

Cartwright frowned. "Let's hope there's not too much of that."

9

Jen yawned as the SUV wound through the Atlanta streets the next morning. She felt the pouch threaded onto her belt for the hundredth time. She unzipped it and pulled out the stoppered syringe. *Can't believe this freaking thing is humanity's last hope.* She returned it, making sure the padding inside was wrapped completely around it.

They'd passed only a few pedestrians and bicyclists, and even fewer vehicles. It had rained overnight and the sun baked the streets, evaporating the puddles.

"I'll be glad to get out of this freaking humidity." Jen pulled her shirt away from her chest.

"Where are all the people?" Zeke asked. "It's like a ghost town."

Agent Rodriguez glanced at him from the front passenger seat. "It's getting worse every day." He cracked his neck. "A week ago we'd had our first major outbreak in Atlanta, but now there are several every day."

"We had a couple in Providence," Wayne said, "but the rest of Rhode Island has been pretty calm."

Zeke examined the cell phone he'd been given at the armory. "No social media. No games. How can they call this a phone?"

"It's for calls only," Wayne said. He sat between Jen and Zeke and his shoulder kept rubbing Jen's as the vehicle bounced over uneven roads.

Jen pulled her phone out. In a hardened case, it was pre-programmed with numbers for Cartwright, Howell, and everyone in the SUV. She rapped her knuckles on the case. "Could run this thing over with a tank and not hurt it."

The SUV swerved and Jen pressed into Wayne. She pulled back and murmured, "Sorry."

Wayne gave her a smile. "No worries."

Stop it, Jen. You've got a job to do. Don't start getting all gooey like in a bad novel. There's still an apocalypse going on.

A breeze caught discarded papers and they flew down the empty street. "Doesn't look like there's anyone left in the city," Wayne said.

"Everyone's holed up in their houses," Daniels said.

The SUV swung around a curve and Jen held onto the door handle to keep from tumbling into Wayne again. Two blocks ahead, a crowd filled the street.

"Looks like we found the party," she said.

"Shit," Rodriguez said. "Everyone stay close to me when we get out. We'll have to get through that mess."

Jen frowned. "I'm not comfortable with crowds right now."

Daniels looked at Rodriguez. "They're all trying to get on the train. It's the only reliable long-distance transportation unless you walk or bike." Rodriguez put a hand on the SUV driver's arm. "Stop here, Stan."

The vehicle pulled to the curb. The crowd's edge lay a hundred feet ahead.

Rodriguez turned to the others. "There's no time to be polite. We'll have to bull through. I'll lead and Daniels will take the rear. Stay with us and have your badges out when we get to the train."

"I don't have a badge," Wayne said.

"Stick close. We'll get you in," Daniels said.

Jen lined up behind Rodriguez, followed by Zeke and Wayne. Daniels called out from behind her. "Ready."

Rodriguez stepped into the milling crowd, holding his badge up. "Excuse me. Homeland Security. Let us pass."

Jen stayed on his ass as he wove through the mass of humanity. Halfway there, she glanced over her shoulder and was reassured that the others still followed close behind.

A woman's scream came from the top of the wide gradual steps leading into the terminal. Yelling and cursing followed, and the crowd converged on the spot, jostling and shoving. A fight broke out.

Someone slammed into Jen from her left and she stumbled, but managed to stay upright. *Don't want to fall in this mess.*

Rodriguez yelled over his shoulder, "We're gonna have to take a detour. This way."

He pushed to the left, and Jen glimpsed the crowd ten yards ahead. The people appeared calmer.

The fighting spilled down the steps like a wave washing over the mass of hot, sweaty Atlantans. Rammed again, Jen was shoved into a tall, beefy man who glared at her. He grabbed her arm and pulled her toward him. "Who the hell do you think you are?"

"You'll find out when I knee your balls up into your throat," Jen said. She tried to follow through on the threat but the mob was pressed so close together, she had no room to act.

Someone grabbed her other arm. Jen glanced over. Wayne had stretched out and clenched her upper arm. Zeke peered at her over his shoulder. He reached back and pulled his katana, but he might as well have left it in its scabbard for all the good he could do with it.

The beefy man wrapped one ham-sized hand around Jen's throat. "Just 'cause you're government doesn't make you special."

Jen choked and tried again to knee the asshole, but she was immobilized by the bodies pressing in on her. Dots speckled her vision as she struggled to breathe.

"Jen," Zeke yelled.

An explosion came from nearby and the hand released her. Jen's legs gave out and she collapsed to the ground, her lungs heaving for air.

Wayne lifted her to her feet. "Come on."

Everyone outside the station had hit the ground except the agents, Wayne, Zeke, and Jen. Daniels stood with his gun pointed into the air.

The beefy man stood and pulled a handgun from the small of his back. Rodriguez and Daniels put three bullets each in him before he dropped.

Zeke drew his katana and stepped over cowering civilians. "Can't let him turn."

The beefy man grabbed a young woman's arm and clamped it in his jaw. She screamed, and a two-year-old girl at her side cried.

Jen stepped on people to get to the child and snatched her up. Zeke sliced halfway through the beefy man's neck, but not before he'd bitten two more people.

The crowd panicked and fled for the street. Zeke lopped off the beefy man's head with his next stroke, and Wayne took position next to him with his bat. A teen zombie rushed him and he swung, but his timing was off and the zombie crashed into him, knocking him to the ground.

A well-placed bullet from Agent Daniels exploded out the back of the teen zombie's head. "We can't stay here to help. Our mission is too important."

With the toddler in one arm and her pistol in the other, Jen shot one of the yellow-eyed monsters sizing Wayne up. The baby screamed, tears pouring down its cheeks. "He's right," she yelled. "Zeke. Wayne. I need you with me."

The brothers backed toward her. Zombies sprung on humans in panicked flight.

Shots came from the terminal. Militia members stood in the doorways firing.

Jen followed Rodriguez as he dashed toward the terminal. Chaos reigned. A few gunshots boomed within the crowd, but they were quickly silenced.

The path up the terminal steps cleared as the mob rushed for the streets. Rodriguez bull-rushed up the steps and slammed into a thin middle-aged man with luminescent yellow eyes, knocking him to the side. Jen side-stepped a zombie and its throatless victim and ducked through the terminal door behind Rodriguez.

The train's doors were still open, but a line of armed men, in police uniforms and civilian clothes, blocked the only way through a makeshift fence. Panicked people pushed against it, threatening to knock it down.

Daniels zipped past the others, his badge held high. "Homeland Security. We need to get on this train."

The first of the zombies entered the terminal and clamped its teeth on an older man's shoulder. The crowd inside surged away from them, and many rushed the side entrances in a desperate attempt to escape.

"Path is clear," Rodriguez yelled.

Jen hugged the child tightly and sprinted for the gate.

Several rifles pointed at the group as they made the gate.

Rodriguez and Daniels shoved their badges against the chain links. "Homeland Security," Rodriguez said. "We have to be on that train."

A state trooper jogged over and glanced at the badges. "Let 'em in."

A man in cammies with no insignia lifted the latch and opened the gate.

More zombies surged through the doors. The men protecting the train opened fire. Jen cringed. The explosive sounds echoed off the walls.

Civilians behind the fence were lined up to enter the train. Rodriguez barreled through them, and Jen panted, trying to keep up.

The guard at the head of the line looked up as they approached. "Back in line."

Rodriguez showed his badge. "We're going on. You have thirty seconds to get as many of these people as you can on board and then this train is leaving."

Jen pushed past the guard and ran into the first car. A few startled passengers looked up.

"When are we going?" asked a thirty-something woman with short platinum-blonde hair and a Georgia twang.

Jen took a seat. The child, a girl, kept her face buried into Jen's shoulder.

Zeke and Wayne hopped on and took positions at the door. Both had their rifles aimed toward the gate. Zeke fired. Wayne glanced at him. "Now?" he asked.

"You don't wait for orcs to be slicing you up before you start swinging your sword," Zeke yelled.

Rodriguez zipped into the car, his eyes searching for something.

Daniels backed into the car, his pistol out and firing. "They're breaching the damn fence."

Got to help.

Jen tried to lower the child to the seat, but she whimpered and clamped her arms around Jen's neck.

Three figures darted into the car just as the doors closed. One barreled into Zeke, knocking him to the floor, another attacked the platinum blonde, and the third landed facedown in the aisle next to Jen.

The zombie in the aisle sprung to its feet and gaped at Jen and the girl with its hungry yellow eyes.

10

The zombie on top of Zeke was almost a mirror image of him. Its hair half dyed in blue and half in red made its yellow eyes seem almost stylish.

Jen pulled the little girl's arms from her neck and pushed her away from the aisle. The zombie from the aisle hit Jen full force before she could fire. Her gun hand flung back, slamming into the wall. Pain exploded in her wrist and the gun dropped to the floor.

Jen held the zombie back with a forearm across the throat, but the barrel-chested man was bigger and heavier than her. He snapped his jaws and lunged at the same time.

She kneed him in the crotch as hard as she could and the zombie lunged again. *Damn. They don't feel that?*

A hand grasped the zombie's shoulder and spun it around. Wrist throbbing, Jen fished her tomahawk from its sheath.

Wayne had the zombie by the shirt and reared back with the bat, but the zombie was too fast and tackled him onto the seat across the aisle. Wayne shoved the bat handle into the zombie's mouth, but it didn't let up.

Jen glanced to make sure the girl was all right, then brought the pointed end of the tomahawk down toward the back of the zombie's head. It moved at the last second, and the point ended up buried in its shoulder.

"Shit."

Jen yanked the weapon from its shoulder and swung again, planting the point firmly in the creature's skull. It collapsed on top of Wayne.

Zeke still wrestled with his attacker. Its teeth were inches from sinking into his throat and his arms trembled with the strain of holding it back. *He's not going to last.*

The platinum blonde had turned and tore a chunk of meat from a teenage boys arm before turning and leering at the little girl.

Shit. Zeke's about to bite it, but I can't let that monster bite the girl, either.

Jen grabbed the barrel-chested zombie and yanked it off Wayne. "Help Zeke."

Without waiting for an answer, she spun, bringing the tomahawk overhead, and sliced the platinum blonde's arm. Less than a foot from the girl, the blonde turned and hissed at Jen.

Pandemonium broke out in the front of the car as the teenage boy turned and attacked several other passengers.

This shit's getting out of hand. Jen lowered her shoulder and rammed the platinum blonde to the side. It stumbled, then leapt. Jen ducked and straightened as the zombie landed on her. She catapulted the blonde into the wall, where it fell to the floor, stunned.

The little girl shrank against the wall between the seats. A quick glance toward Zeke showed Wayne knocking the snot out of the zombie's skull with the bat.

Jen fell upon the blonde and chopped at its head with

the blade. Once, twice, three times. Her lungs burned with the effort. Blood splattered in her eyes, and she stepped back and wiped them with her sleeves.

The blonde lay in an unmoving heap.

Rodriguez ran to the other end of the car and picked up a phone cradled on the wall. "Engineer? This is Agent Rodriguez of Homeland Security. You are ordered to get us the hell out of here."

A man slammed into the outside of the door, his eyes wide in panic. He clawed the edge, straining to pull on it. It took a second for Jen to recognize the state trooper.

A large woman in a torn and bloody floral print dress grabbed him from behind. She twisted his head and sank her teeth into his cheek. Blood sprayed the glass on the car door as she ripped flesh and muscle from the trooper.

"Start this fucking thing now," Rodriguez screamed into the phone.

The train jerked, almost knocking Rodriguez off his feet, and it slowly made its way down the track.

The platform was blood-splattered carnage. No one was left alive. Dozens of zombies rushed the train but fell away as it pulled out of the station.

Jen lifted the girl onto the seat and let her wrap her arms around her neck again. Zeke and Wayne sat on the floor in the corner and leaned against the wall, catching their breath. The bloody remnants of their zombie lay in front of them.

Daniels stood over the third zombie, a bullet wound in its temple.

Of the six passengers that were already in the train car when Jen arrived, only two still breathed. One, a boy barely in his teens, stood in the corner with glassy eyes and a trembling lip.

Across from him a burly guy in biker colors and a porn star mustache stood over two dead zombies. Blood dripped from a machete he held. He cracked his neck. "Don't usually get my workout so early in the morning."

Zeke stood and stepped over bodies to get to the biker. He held out a fist for the biker to bump. "I'm feeling ya. My name's Zeke, and I'm a ninja."

Biker Guy glared at Zeke from beneath bushy brows, his grip tightening on the machete handle.

Zeke lowered his arm and backed away. "We're cool."

Rodriguez sat on a bloodied seat and talked on the phone.

"Who's he talking to?" Jen asked.

Daniels wiped his hands on his suit coat. "Cartwright."

Wayne pushed past Daniels and approached the boy. "You OK, buddy?"

The boy remained quiet.

Wayne took a knee in front of the boy. "I'm Wayne. What's your name?"

The boy's gaze rose to meet Wayne's. "Jamarcus."

He pointed to a thirty-something man sprawled at Biker Guy's feet. "That's Uncle Floyd."

Biker Guy licked his lips and moved away from the body.

"I'm sorry about your uncle," Wayne said.

Not only hot, but Wayne's a saint, too? I feel like I'm stuck in the Hallmark movie from hell.

Jen's heart ached for the boy.

Rodriguez snapped his phone shut and stood. "Listen up. Cartwright's getting resources in New York to meet us when we stop. They'll quarantine the train and go through it car by car, but we'll be the first car."

"Who's Cartwright?" Biker Guy asked. "For that matter, who are you suits?"

"Homeland Security agents," Jen said. "All of us. And Cartwright's someone who can get shit done."

Biker Guy eyed her up and down as if he'd just noticed her.

"I'll vouch for you," Jen said. "You'll get out of here with us."

Daniels' eyebrows rose and he exchanged a glance with Rodriguez, who shrugged.

Biker Guy nodded. "You're a helluva fighter. What's your name?"

"Jen. Jen Reed. And yours?"

"Call me D-Day."

Zeke smiled. "That's so cool. I want a name like that."

"D-Day?" Jen asked.

D-Day wiped a smear of blood off his forehead. "Did I stutter?"

He grunted and sat on a dry section of seat, facing away from the others.

Guess he's done talking.

Jen checked the serum. *Still there. Still intact.*

She sat next to the girl the rest of the way to New York City. She never said a word, even though Jen tried to get her name.

The train rolled into the station. Armed law enforcement lined the platform, while a set of armed men in civilian clothes, each wearing a red arm band, stood in a group to the side. *Militia. There has to be a hundred of them.*

When the train stopped, the militia members disappeared toward the rear cars. A squad of armed men dressed in black with helmets and vests approached their car, their rifles up and ready.

Rodriguez stood at the door and pressed his badge to it. "Agent Rodriguez," he yelled through the glass.

The SWAT leader spoke into a mic clipped to his shoulder, and a few seconds later, the door whooshed open.

Rodriguez stumbled back as the squad rushed the car. Calls of "all clear" came from the SWAT members as they fanned out in the car.

A man in a blue jacket with the letters FBI on it stepped in. "Agent Rodriguez?"

Rodriguez raised his hand, then pointed at Daniels. "Agent Daniels."

The FBI agent nodded. "I'm Hess. All the rest are with you?"

"All except the kids and the biker," Rodriguez said.

Hess stepped out the door and waved another agent over. "Get these kids to DCS."

The little girl clutched Jen's neck so tight, she coughed. Prying the girl's arms away, Jen said, "Come on, honey. These people will take care of you."

Tears rolled down the girl's face as the agent took her. She screamed, "I want to stay with you. I want to be safe."

Jen swallowed and dropped her gaze to the floor. *I'm the last person to be around if you want to be safe.*

11

Hess led them to another platform, where a line of people waited to board a train.

"This looks a lot more organized than Atlanta," Jen said.

Hess nodded. "We have a ton of people wanting to get on, but we preprocess them a couple of blocks away. Only those who are boarding are allowed in the station."

He walked right up the line to the front, where a couple of militia men with red armbands stood cradling AK-47 style guns.

"National security," he said. "These folks go on first."

One of the militia men eyed D-Day. "The big guy doesn't look government to me."

D-Day stared the guy down and cracked his knuckles.

"He's with us," Rodriguez said.

There's a surprise.

Rodriguez gave Jen a slight nod.

"We can't fit him in this car," Hess said, "but we'll get him a seat a few cars back." He called a militia man over and pointed at D-Day. "Get the big guy in the closest car to number one that you can."

"Yes, sir." The militia man led D-Day farther down the line of cars.

An older couple stood at the front of the line. The lady was shooting daggers at the group with her eyes. "We paid to be here," she said. "It's a shame some people don't know their place."

This bitch would make a good zombie.

One of the militiamen guarding the train pointed to the first car. "Go on in," he said to Rodriguez.

Rodriguez waved them on. Zeke pushed past the old couple and gave the lady one of his patented silly grins. She scowled.

They entered the car and Jen plopped onto the back seat and adjusted the serum bag on her belt. Zeke went to sit next to her, but Wayne slipped in first. Zeke frowned and took the seat in front of them.

He turned around, his arm on the back of the seat. "Do you think we'll see some action up north?"

Jen sighed. "I hope not. Shit's stressful enough as it is. I wish I knew how it's going on the front."

Zeke shrugged. "Call Howell."

"Howell?" Wayne asked.

"He's our contact at the Pentagon," Jen said. "He'll give us the straight poop."

Rodriguez and Daniels took seats on either side of the aisle in the middle of the car. They leaned across the aisle and spoke in low tones.

"Are you going to call him?" Wayne asked.

Jen broke from her thoughts. "Who?"

"Howell," Zeke said. "We were just talking about him."

"Oh, yeah." Jen pulled her cell phone from her pants

pocket and flipped it open. She scrolled down the list of pre-programmed contacts. All the members of the team were listed as well as Cartwright, Mark, and Howell.

She highlighted Howell's name and pressed the Call button. It rang on the other end.

A click, then "Howell here."

"Sergeant Howell, it's Jen."

"Jen. I heard you had a hard time getting out of Atlanta."

Jen laughed. "Nothing compared to making our exit from Spokane."

"I heard that," Howell said. His voice became serious. "I've got a ton of shit going on here, what can I do for you?"

Jen swallowed. "What are we headed into?"

"In Boston? Big city with some small outbreaks here and there, but they've been keeping the lid on it."

"That wasn't a small outbreak in Atlanta," Jen said. "I saw how it started, and it spread faster than Big Bertha's ass at an all-you-can-eat buffet. I don't want to imagine it happening like that elsewhere."

Howell didn't answer.

"Howell, you still there?"

His voice lowered. "I'm seeing that same pattern. I know the brass are worried about it, but they can't break any forces off to go back east and deal with it. Did you know Boise and Las Vegas fell?"

Shit. "But what if we have an outbreak here that can't be put down?"

"Then we're lost," Howell said.

Jen frowned. *If I didn't know Howell, I'd think he's losing hope.* "I'll get this serum where it's supposed to go and we'll shut this shit down before it gets too bad."

"We're all counting on you, Jen," Howell said. "Let me know if there's anything I can do for you. I have access to local law enforcement reports, satellite images, and intel reports."

"Will do."

"And Jen, keep me updated. Don't bother Dr. Cartwright. Call me instead."

Really?

"OK. Talk to you later." The call ended.

Zeke peered at her over the back of the seat. "So what did he say?"

"Hordes are still making gains out west and there've have been flare-ups in the east like what we saw in Atlanta."

Zeke smiled. "More zombies to kill."

Wayne raised an eyebrow. "You actually looking forward to that, little brother?"

Zeke turned back around.

Heat rose in Jen's face. She elbowed Wayne in the side. He flinched. "What the hell?"

"Your little brother saved me more times than I can count," she said. "He's trying to keep his head in the game, so don't fuck him up."

Wayne gazed into her eyes, then said, "I can protect you."

"Oh, great. The big testosterone-fueled man is going to protect little old me." She poked a finger in his chest. "I've killed far more zombies than you've ever seen. Maybe I should protect you."

Wayne's lips pressed together and he looked away.

"I said Zeke saved me," Jen said. "I didn't say he protected me. We protected each other, and so did a lot of other people. Most of them are dead."

She sat back in her seat and crossed her arms. *Welcome to the real world, dude.*

Passengers boarded. The first were the old couple. They took the first seat on the right. The lady placed a coat-draped case between them. She glanced back and her eyes met Jen's. The old bag scowled and turned away.

What's she got in that box? Gold bricks? Or maybe something more valuable like a personality?

Zeke was twisted around in his seat, facing her. "Can't wait to get going, but there are still empty seats."

"I wonder how many seats are in this car," Jen said.

"Sixty-two," Zeke replied.

"Now how the hell did you know that?"

"I counted when we came in."

A thirty-something balding man with an enormous beer gut and a scowl led a mousy woman to the seat across from the old couple. "In here, honey," he said as he guided her to the seat.

The woman's eyes darted back and forth. It looked like a loud cough would be enough to send her into a panic.

Perfect person to be with in a zombie apocalypse.

The old lady up front surveyed her fellow passengers, most dressed in casual clothes. She whispered something to her husband.

Poor rich bitch has to put up with the rabble.

The doors whooshed closed and the murmur of conversation picked up in the car. Rodriguez and Daniels broke off their conversation and sat back in their seats.

A voice crackled from the speakers. "Ladies and Gentlemen, this is your conductor. We are about to begin our journey to Boston, Massachusetts, with stops in between. All cars are full to capacity and all seats taken, so please remain in yours. Nonessential cars have been replaced with passenger cars for maximum capacity, so there are no food and beverage services on this route."

"No beer?" Beer Belly wailed.

The train jerked and rumbled from the station. Breaking

into daylight, it picked up speed. Jen looked out the window, squinting her eyes in the light. She jostled shoulder to shoulder with Wayne, but neither of them spoke.

The train rolled through the city and picked up speed. Several passengers leaned back and closed their eyes.

This'll be a piece of cake at this rate.

The conductor burst in from the next car and spoke in hushed tones to Agent Rodriguez. Rodriguez picked up the direct line to the engineer and listened. He pulled the phone from his ear and looked at the conductor, shaking his head.

So much for the piece of cake.

The conductor disappeared into the next car and Jen caught Rodriguez's gaze and shrugged.

Rodriguez beckoned Daniels over and whispered something to him. Daniels frowned.

Jen jumped up and made a beeline to the two agents. "What's going on?"

Daniels motioned for her to lower her voice. "Don't want to panic anyone."

"The engineer's not answering his intercom," Rodriguez said.

"Is that unusual?" Jen asked.

"According to the conductor, the only time that's ever happened was when the intercom wasn't working or the engineer had a medical emergency. Since they did a successful sound check before they left, he's concerned for the engineer."

"What have you got in there?" Beer Belly's booming voice filled the cab.

He stood in the aisle glaring down at the old lady, who cringed away from him. Beer Belly pointed at the covered case between the old lady and the old man. "There's something alive in there."

Rodriguez and Daniels exchanged a glance, and Daniels strode toward the front.

Passengers craned their necks to get a view of the disruption at the front of the car.

"Mind your own business," the old lady snapped. "You don't know what you're talking about."

"Oh, I don't, do I?" Beer Belly lunged and grabbed the case. The older couple latched onto it like their lives depended on it.

"Help," the old lady screamed.

Daniels reached Beer Belly and put a hand on his shoulder. "Let it go and sit down."

Beer Belly let go of the case. "Who the hell do you think you are?"

The old lady and the old man fell backward with the suddenly freed case. It slammed into the wall and fell to the floor.

Jen stood to see. The coat had fallen off and exposed a plastic animal carrier with a wire frame door. The door had popped open and something inside stirred.

With a deep growl a bloodied cat with piercing yellow eyes sprung from the carrier and landed on Beer Belly's thigh. He screamed when the cat bit through his pants and shredded his leg.

12

Daniels stumbled backward and the old lady let out a wail. "My Buttons. Don't hurt my fur baby."

Beer Belly swatted the cat off his leg, tripped, and fell onto his seat. His wife shrank against the wall.

The cat leapt onto Daniels' chest and clawed his suit. Daniels pulled his pistol and bashed the cat with the butt, knocking it to the floor, where it skittered underneath a seat.

Passengers pulled their legs from the floor and stood on their seats while the old lady went to her knees and crawled down the aisle. "Here, Buttons. Mommy's here."

The old man stumbled, clutching his chest, then collapsed out of sight.

Jen pushed past Wayne. "See if you can bash the cat."

She pulled her tomahawk while Wayne picked up his bat and Zeke unsheathed his katana.

"Not a lot of room in here to swing," Zeke said.

Beer Belly's wife screeched as her husband pounced on her, pinning her to the wall. He clamped his teeth on her throat and her cries died in a gurgle as he shook his head and ripped her throat out.

A gunshot went off and the back of Beer Belly's head disintegrated. He fell off the seat and sprawled on the floor.

The cat sprang onto a woman's chest and bit her shoulder. Jen charged and swung at the zombie cat. It leapt onto another passenger, and Jen's blade ended up in the wounded lady's neck. "Shit!"

The lady's cloudy eyes turned to Jen. *Already turning.*

Jen freed the blade, twisted the handle, and slammed the pointed end into the lady's temple. She dropped to the floor.

Zeke stood at the back, his katana at the ready, but he didn't attack. *He's afraid of hitting someone uninfected.*

Beer Belly's wife jumped on a twenty-something man's back and bit into the back of his neck while the old man had turned and proceeded to peel the flesh from his wife's cheek.

"Daniels," Rodriguez yelled.

Daniels stood in the middle of it all, his back to Jen. He spun when his name was called, and drool spilled from his mouth as he eyed a meal.

Rodriguez fired, the bullet entering Daniels' eye and spraying blood, flesh, and bone as it exited from the back of his skull.

The cat jumped onto the seat in front of Jen, its gaze locked on her. A flash from the corner of her eye, and an aluminum bat slammed into the spot the cat had been a second earlier.

"This shit's out of hand," Jen said. She raced to the door to the next car and grabbed the handle. Through the window, nervous passengers stood and stared at her.

She jerked the door open. "In here. Now."

Wayne slammed the bat into a charging zombie, hitting it in the ribs and knocking it to the side. Jen grabbed his shirt collar and yanked him off balance. "Leave it."

He stumbled into the next car and Jen followed. Zeke rushed in and Rodriguez stood at the doorway, firing wildly.

The passengers in the second car screamed and mobbed the back door.

Several zombies rushed Rodriguez, one up the aisle, two more leaping from neighboring seats.

Halfway through the door, he pulled the trigger and his gun clicked empty. He stumbled backward and slammed the door, but two bloodied arms prevented it from closing all the way.

The passengers bottlenecked at the back door. Jen grasped Wayne's arm and pointed at the fleeing passengers. "Help them out. We need the way clear in case we have to retreat farther. Make sure you keep the door propped open."

Wayne nodded and dashed to the back of the car.

Jen rushed to help Rodriguez. She chopped at one of the intruding arms, but it didn't withdraw and the door pushed wider a couple of inches.

Zeke struck the best he could with the limited room, but it did little good.

His teeth gritted and face red, Rodriguez strained to keep the door from flying open. "You go," he said. "We need you to make it to Boston."

"You can't let this door go and get to the next car in time," Jen yelled.

"I know."

"We're clear." Wayne stood at the back door. The last of the passengers were already halfway through the third car.

Jen pointed to Wayne. "Let's go, Zeke."

Jen dashed down the aisle and through the door. She turned just as Zeke made it into the car. The door Rodriguez held had opened more than two feet. Two zombies had pushed their upper bodies partially in, and more arms had snaked their way through, putting pressure on the door.

Rodriguez gave a groan and collapsed. A zombie wave poured over him and into the car.

Jen shut the door and it latched. Seconds later several zombies slammed into it, smearing the window in blood.

Jen turned to the others. "That's one solid-ass door—"

Zeke and Wayne stood halfway down the aisle battling five zombies.

What the hell?

Jen unholstered her pistol and shot at a zombie in a beanie cap missing half its face. Rushing Wayne, it fell back as the bullet slammed into its chest, but quickly recovered.

Jen grasped the pistol in both hands and took a deep breath, then held it. She squeezed the trigger, absorbing the satisfying recoil and the sight of what remained of the zombie's face collapsing around its nose.

Wayne pounded the temple of another zombie with the bat and Zeke made an abbreviated slash with the katana and left a teen goth zombie with its neck halfway severed.

"Where they hell did they come from?" Jen yelled.

A blur zipped from her right, and she ducked just as the zombie cat sailed over her. *Son of a bitch!*

She holstered the pistol and yanked the tomahawk from its sheath as she scanned for the devil cat. "Where the hell did you go?"

Her eyes fell on the open door to the next car. "Tell me it isn't chasing the rest of the passengers."

She rushed the aisle, slashing and knocking zombies to the side. Wayne cracked the skull of a woman who collapsed back into two other zombies.

"Keep moving," Jen yelled. "Almost there."

Something grabbed her arm and she jerked back as a heavy man with a bloodied eye socket dipped his head to take a chunk out of her. Kicking out, she connected with one of his knees. He lost his balance and Jen threw him backward. He fell onto the floor in the doorway, blocking access to the fourth car. Jen brought the tomahawk overhead and jammed the point through the zombie's good eye and into his brain. He went limp.

Lungs heaving, Jen leaned on the doorway and looked into the fourth car. The outbreak had spread there and she faced more than twenty fresh zombies.

Wayne and Zeke had reached her. Eight more zombies pursued them, all the rest having been destroyed or moved into the next car.

"Change of plans," Jen yelled. "We stay in this car. Take the rest of them out."

Zeke stepped next to Jen. "Stay back." He pressed into the remaining zombies, his katana a blur around him. No longer worried about hitting a human, he spun, swung, and danced down the aisle, thinning out the remaining zombies until only one remained.

A shot took that one down, and Wayne stood behind Zeke with his pistol pointed at the zombie and a smile on his face.

More zombies entered the fourth car from the back and rushed up the aisle as Jen tried to close the door, but the heavy zombie she'd killed blocked the door from closing.

"Look," Zeke yelled.

Jen turned back to the third car. The old man was fumbling with the door latch.

"The old man's a fucking leader," Jen yelled.

The door between the second and third cars slid open and the horde burst through.

13

The old man lurched into the second car, his intense yellow gaze on Jen. She grabbed the dead zombie blocking their escape. "Help me."

Zeke and Wayne pitched in and they rolled the zombie out of the way.

Zeke ran into the fourth car and took a stance halfway down the aisle. Jen pushed Wayne through. "Back him up."

Wayne raced down the aisle and Jen stepped into the car, closing the door behind her. The horde up front held back, and the old man stumbled toward the door.

"Oh, hell no." Jen pulled her pistol and let the old man get closer. When he was only fifteen feet away, she slid the door open a foot and propped her gun against it for stability. A quick aim and a squeeze and she hit the old man in the neck. The horde roared and pushed forward.

Sweat pouring down her back, Jen aimed again. The horde had just about reached the old man and would be on her in a few seconds. Time slowed. Jen lined up the sights and held her breath. Fighting the urge to hurry, she squeezed slow enough to make sure she didn't pull the sights off target.

The pistol boomed and recoiled. A hole appeared in the old man's forehead and Jen leaned back, slamming the door shut. Three fingers made it through the doorway and were sliced off when the door closed.

The horde roared and banged on the door. Jen gave them the finger and spun to help out Zeke and Wayne.

Her breath hitched as she took in the scene. Zeke and Wayne stood side by side in the middle of the car. Waves of zombies pushed forward, the seats the only thing keeping them from sweeping over the brothers.

Jen aimed at a middle-aged woman in a bloodied pantsuit and put a bullet in her temple.

Wayne knocked back a zombie climbing over a seat.

Zeke beheaded a young man charging down the aisle, then spun and sliced at a teen goth girl who'd climbed on the back of a seat and squatted there like a gargoyle on a medieval church.

Jen shot another zombie about to reach Wayne. *We are so screwed.*

She holstered the pistol and drew the tomahawk. Darting forward, she planted her blade into a one-armed zombie's forehead. Stunned, but still undead, it struggled to its feet and Jen finished it off with a second blow to the same spot.

Another zombie pushed up the aisle between Jen and Zeke. Zeke was locked in a struggle with a wiry, athletic zombie coming over the seat. It had avoided the swings of his katana, but was kept off balance and unable to attack.

Jen took on the aisle zombie and swung sideways with the tomahawk, planting the pointed end in the zombie's temple. It dropped like its strings had been cut, but took the tomahawk with it.

No time to get it.

She yanked the pistol from its holster and shot the two closest zombies point-blank in the head. She shoved one on top of the other, which slowed a third that was creeping up on her.

Too many. Getting tired.

A booming voice came from the other end of the car. "Work your way to me."

Jen looked up. D-Day's head and shoulders towered over the zombies, his machete rythmically mowing down the undead.

She retrieved her tomahawk and attacked with new energy. *Maybe we can get through.*

The bodies had stacked up in the aisle, which kept the zombies from rushing them full force, but also blocked Jen's way forward.

"We can't get them all," D-Day said. "Make your move now. Straight down the middle."

Zeke hopped onto the pile of bodies blocking the way and took out two zombies climbing over. His eyes were wide and maniacal and his face was splattered in blood.

Jen ran to Wayne. "Follow Zeke. I'll be right behind."

Wayne shook his head. "I'll take the rear and cover you."

Here comes the freaking testosterone. "I need you to help clear the way with Zeke. The rear is easy. Is that what you want to do?"

Wayne pursed his lips, then dashed to join Zeke. He leapt onto the body pile and jumped off with the bat over his head. He landed next to Zeke, the bat crushing a redheaded zombie's skull.

D-Day reached the brothers. Both of his bare arms were

wrapped in clothing and taped. He used them to push back snapping zombies. Even when one latched onto his arm, its teeth didn't penetrate to the skin.

Smart idea.

D-Day glared at her. "Now."

Jen raced toward the others. She jumped onto the pile of bodies and used it as a springboard to leap down the aisle, avoiding several zombies spilling in from the seats.

D-Day turned and rumbled toward the back door like a human plow, his forearms pushing back the remaining undead.

Jen split one zombie's skull and avoided another's grasp as she hurried to catch up.

D-Day reached the back door and yanked it open. Zeke and Wayne sprinted through the door.

Six feet away, D-Day yelled, "Duck."

He swung the machete at Jen's head and she dove for the floor, tumbling through the doorway. She slammed into Wayne's shins, taking him down.

A zombie woman's head rolled in behind her and came to a stop between her outstretched legs.

D-Day slashed another zombie across the face, then backed into the car and slammed the door shut.

The zombies piled up at the door. Jen stood and brushed off her pants. "Thanks. Good thing for us you were on board."

He shrugged. "First thing I saw was people running down the aisle. It was like a cattle stampede. I looked to see what scared them and this car had a bunch of zombies tearing into people."

He patted his sheathed machete. "Figure I'd take a few of 'em out then join the cattle, but that's when I saw you guys."

Zeke sheathed his katana. "Maybe we should just stay in here. Both doors are secure."

A low rumbling came from beneath the seats. It grew into a maniacal growl, then a figure streaked across the aisle and disappeared under the seats on the left.

Jen hefted her tomahawk. "That fucking cat. That's what caused this shit storm."

"Then we've got to kill it." D-Day raised his machete.

"I'll get it." Wayne crept down the aisle, his bat cocked over his shoulder.

"Wait," Jen said. "We need to do this together."

The cat sprang at Wayne and he swung wildly, clipping the cat and knocking it back between the seats.

Wayne scrambled back to the others, his eyes wide. "Damn, that thing is fast."

Zeke kept his eyes on the seats. "How do you want to do this?"

Jen took a deep breath. "Zeke, you and I will each take a side of the aisle. We climb over one seat at a time together."

She pulled her pistol and handed it to D-Day. "Get down on the floor with the pistol. If the cat tries going underneath, take it out."

Wayne looked at her. "What do you want me to do?"

Now there's an attitude change.

"Stand back with D-Day and watch the aisle. In case D-Day misses, you're his backup if it charges him."

"I don't miss," D-Day said.

Jen climbed onto the first seat on the left. The next seat was clear, but she couldn't see all of the third seat.

Zeke crouched on the seat on the right, his eyes surveying the tops of the seats in front of him.

"Anything, D-Day?" Jen asked.

D-Day lay on his side with his back to the door and the pistol in his outstretched hands. "It ain't on the floor."

Jen caught Wayne's eyes. He nodded. "Ready."

"Next seat." Jen stepped onto the next seat as Zeke did the same across the aisle.

"I'm clear," she said.

"Same," Zeke said.

"Next seat," Jen said.

Jen froze as her lead foot touched the seat. She held up her free hand and listened.

A soft purring came from somewhere ahead. "Is that on my side?"

Zeke squinted and tilted his head. "Can't tell, but it's not far off."

"Still nothing on the floor," D-Day said.

Jen's heart pounded and her mouth went dry. *Is this it? Am I going to be taken out by a cat?*

She brought her other foot over and stood on the seat. Nothing in the next seat. She looked at Zeke and he shook his head.

"Next seat," she said.

With a high-pitched growl, the cat launched itself at Zeke's face. He ducked and brought his sword up. The cat sailed over him and missed the blade by a half inch. It landed on the floor in the aisle, then sprung at Jen without hesitating.

A shot went off and Jen flinched. The yellow-eyed beast sailed through the air, its claws out stretched.

Jen brought the tomahawk around with all her strength, but it would be seconds too late.

The silver barrel of an aluminum bat flashed by Jen's face, barely missing her, and slammed into the cat, sending it flying into the wall, where it hit with a crack and fell to the floor.

Another gunshot. "Got it," D-Day yelled.

Jen plopped to the seat and put a hand to her face. *That was too fucking close.*

Wayne stood over her, concern in his eyes. "Are you OK?"

Jen nodded. "Yeah. I'm good."

He nodded and turned.

"Thanks," Jen said.

He looked back at her and smiled. "We all watch out for each other, right?"

She found herself smiling back. "Right."

He held out a hand and she took it and pulled herself up. They stood face-to-face a few inches apart. His eyes were a deeper hazel up close.

He leaned toward her and her heart picked up again, but not from fear, not from exertion. His lips were inches away from hers. She closed her eyes in anticipation.

"Jen," D-Day said.

She blinked and stepped back from Wayne. *What the hell was I thinking? About to make out with a guy in the middle of a zombie apocalypse? It's like a bad movie.*

She turned to D-Day. "What's up?"

He pointed to her waist. "Didn't you have a pouch belted around you?"

Jen followed his gaze. The pouch with the serum was gone.

14

"The serum," she shouted. She checked the seats she'd climbed over and examined every inch of the floor.

"Fuck," she screamed.

"So it was important?" D-Day asked.

Zeke put his head in his hands. "Only the cure for the zombie virus."

"A cure?" D-Day said. "Then why the hell did Jen have it?"

"It's not the cure," Jen said, "but the closest thing to it. I was bringing it to a research lab in Boston to finish it."

Wayne put an arm around her shoulders. "Do you know where you lost it?"

She pushed away from him. "If I did, I would've known that I'd lost it. It could be anywhere in the cars ahead of us."

"Anywhere there are zombies," D-Day said.

Jen's phone rang. "Great. What's next?"

She flipped the phone open and put it to her ear. "Yeah?"

"Jen?" Cartwright's voice hit her like a ton of bricks. *Does this woman have a sixth sense about bad news?*

"Dr. Cartwright," Jen said.

Zeke's eyebrows shot up. Jen put the phone on speaker.

"What's the situation?" Cartwright asked. "Agent Rodriguez was supposed to check with me every hour."

"Rodriguez and Daniels are dead."

"What?"

Jen took a deep breath and let it out. "There was an outbreak on the train. Both Rodriguez and Daniels gave up their lives to keep me safe."

"And you're safe now?" Cartwright asked.

The best thing to do with Cartwright is tell her the truth up front. "We are right now, but we're going to have to go back into the infected cars. The strap on the pouch must've broken during the fighting. The pouch with the serum is in one of those cars."

The phone went silent except for Cartwright's soft breathing.

At least she didn't have a heart attack.

"You must retrieve it," Cartwright said.

No shit. Why didn't I think of that? "We're trying to figure out the best way to do that."

"Hold on," Cartwright said.

The phone clicked, then a tired voice said, "Howell here."

"Sergeant Howell," Cartwright said, "we need your help with the serum."

"Not sure what I can do," Howell said.

"We had an outbreak on our train," Jen said. "The first three cars are full of zombies and the serum is in there."

Howell's voice picked up. "Let me get a railroad contact on."

Another click. Jen looked at Wayne and he shrugged. Zeke was cleaning the blade of his katana on a discarded sweatshirt, while D-Day sat on the edge of a seat staring out the window.

"Jen?"

"Here."

"There are direct-line phones on the wall of each car. Pick it up and the engineer will answer."

"They've already tried that," Cartwright said. "The engineer isn't answering."

"Hold," Howell said.

He came back a minute later. "Railroad communications can't raise him, either. This is a bigger problem than just the serum."

"What do you mean?" Wayne asked.

"Boston is the end of the track. If that train comes in at its current speed, it'll crash and release the zombies in the middle of Boston."

"That's irrelevant," Cartwright said. "If it crashes, it could destroy the serum."

"Are there any surviving passengers?" Howell asked.

"We're not sure," D-Day said. "A bunch of them fled to the back, but we had a zombie cat going around biting people. This whole train could be full of undead."

Cartwright cleared her throat. "Who is that who just spoke?"

"D-Day," Jen said. "Without him, we wouldn't have survived."

"I've got you identified by satellite," Howell said. "You have some low bridges on your route that are over bodies of water. You can jump off into the water."

"But not without the serum," Cartwright said.

"I'm open to suggestions," Jen said.

D-Day stood. "Stop the train and open the doors. The

zombies will wander off and we can go through the cars and find the pouch."

"Then we start the train back up and head to Boston," Wayne said. "But how do we run the train?"

Zeke smiled. "From the engine. We climb on the roof of the cars and walk right over the zombies to the engine."

Jen exchanged a glance with D-Day. The crazy-ass biker grinned. *He's eating this shit up.*

"Can you do it?" Howell asked.

Jen shrugged. "As good an idea as any."

"There's a station in Kingston, Rhode Island," Howell said. "It's pretty rural and I can alert the state troopers to set up there if you think you can stop it in time."

Wayne shuffled his feet. His head was down, but he'd been listening. "Even if we get to the engine, we don't know how to stop it."

"I'll get an engineer on the line to walk you through it," Howell said.

Jen looked at the others. Zeke grinned and gave her a thumbs-up. Wayne looked her in the eye and nodded. D-Day stood. "I'm up for it."

"Looks like it's a go," Jen said. "We'll let you know when we're in the engine."

"Roger," Howell said. "I'll be ready."

The phone clicked.

"Jen," Cartwright said.

"Yes?"

"Mankind is counting on you." The phone clicked dead.

Jen blew a raspberry. "What a stirring motivational speech."

D-Day pulled the handle for the outside door and slid it open with a whoosh.

Jen held her hands over her ears. "I hadn't realized how much of the noise the cars kept out."

"I'll go first." Zeke approached the door and stuck his head out, the wind making the spikes in his hair bend. The door was at the back end of the car. Zeke held onto the inside of the doorway as he swung the other half of his body out.

Jen's heart skipped a beat as he pulled himself outside. She ran to the door. Zeke was around the back corner of the car. "There are a couple of places to grab," he yelled as the wind battered him and his clothes flapped. "Make sure you have a good grip before you come around."

He looked up. "There are handholds all the way to the roof. Just take it slow and keep your grip." He disappeared around the corner.

Wayne moved to the doorway. "I'll go next." Without another word, he grabbed the inside handhold and swung himself around the outside of the cab. Even faster than Zeke, he disappeared.

D-Day moved next to Jen and grabbed the back of her shirt. "I'll hold you just in case. When you're ready to go around the corner, nod at me and I'll let go."

"Got it."

Jen grasped an inlaid metal handle just inside the doorway and positioned her right foot beneath it. D-Day grabbed her shirt. "Any time you're ready," he said.

Jen took a deep breath and flung her left arm and leg out and around the outside of the car. Her hand slid down the side and ran into a handhold but she couldn't hold on. Her heart banged like a bongo drum as her left side fell from the car. Lifted by the back of her shirt and pulled in, she was able to keep her balance and ended up back in the car.

"Don't know if I can do this," she said.

D-Day's eyebrows lowered. "Bullshit. Don't even think that. Did you feel anything to grab on to?"

She nodded. "About a foot lower than where my hand landed."

"Then now you know what to expect. Go again."

Jen licked her chapped lips. She bent her knees slightly, then leapt. Her hand slapped the smooth metal side of the car and slipped down. She curled her fingers and a split second later they slid into the handhold. She scrambled with her left foot and found a narrow outcropping to prop it on.

Looking up, she saw the handholds Zeke had talked about. Zeke stood on top of the roof and cupped his hands around his mouth. "Don't come up yet. Move to your left so that your right foot and hand are on something stable outside of the car."

Jen nodded. A couple of feet to her left were similar handholds. Jen nodded at D-Day and he released her shirt. She gulped. *No safety net.*

She gingerly brought her right foot to her left, then her right hand to her left. Arms trembling, she concentrated on the handholds on her left and moved her left hand to one and gripped it. Then her left foot to the one below it.

"I've got it," she yelled.

Zeke's beaming face looked down and he clapped, then motioned for her to climb.

Jen grabbed a handhold above with her right hand, pulled herself up, then found another with her left.

She stabilized her feet.

The train hit a sharp corner and Jen slipped, her feet flying out with the centrifugal force of the turn. Hanging only by her fingers, they began to slip.

15

Caught by the wind, Jen's leg's swung out from the train. She gritted her teeth and concentrated on keeping her tenuous grasp.

Her legs slammed into the side of the car again and she winced. *Don't think I can take another one.*

Zeke and Wayne knelt at the edge of the roof, stretching their arms out, but she needed to be a couple feet closer.

Someone grabbed Jen's legs and she looked into D-Day's eyes. He hung out the door with one arm and had the other encircling her legs, preventing them from flopping in the wind.

"I'm going to give you a push," he yelled over the train's racket. "Only one chance for this."

Zeke hollered to her, "When he pushes, reach for our hands."

Jen nodded and looked back at D-Day. Fear froze her.

"You can do this," D-Day said. "You've got more balls than most men I've known. Don't overthink it, just reach for their hands."

Jen took a deep breath and swallowed.

"On the count of three," D-Day bellowed. "One...two...three."

He swung his body around still holding on to the doorway and threw her upwards. She reached out with both arms, and Zeke and Wayne grabbed them as D-Day let go of her legs. Her weight pulled on them and Zeke seemed to slip, but he regained his balance.

They pulled her close and she found footing and pushed as they yanked her to the top of the car.

She lay on her stomach, panting, the wind taking her breath away.

Zeke bent down to her. "You okay?"

She nodded. Wayne put a hand on her back. "Take your time."

She'd regained her breath by the time D-Day pulled himself onto the roof. He helped her stand, but said nothing.

"Thank you," she said. "Thank you all."

"Enough of this bullshit," D-Day said. "Let's get this train stopped."

Zeke led the way, hopping to the next car with ease. Jen recalled him practically flying over the empty space between two buildings in Spokane. *Mine didn't go too well. Good thing these cars are a lot closer together.*

With no more slips, they made it to the first car in minutes. Jen peered over the side.

The door to the engine stood open. A rail above it caught her eye. She pointed. "We can grab that and swing right in."

Zeke squinted his eyes against the wind. "We don't know what's in there. I should go first."

Wayne put a hand on his shoulder. "I should go first this

time. If there are zombies in there, they'll go for me and you can swoop in behind them."

Zeke frowned.

"I don't trust anyone to cover my back more than you," Wayne said.

"OK." Zeke gave one of his grins.

Wayne climbed down to the bar. He squatted, facing the engine, and pushed off. He swung into the door and disappeared.

Zeke scrambled down and mimicked his brother's actions, vanishing inside in one fluid motion.

Wayne stuck his head out. "All clear."

Jen eased her way to the bar and took a minute to compose herself before she swung in. She tumbled onto the floor and stopped just before rolling into the wall. Wayne helped her up, then turned to examine a panel with switches and buttons.

He's stopped asking if I'm OK every few minutes. Maybe he'll work out after all.

D-Day landed on his feet like a cat. A big, hairy cat with lots of muscles.

Zeke pointed at the floor. A wide streak of blood painted it to the doorway. "Guess we know what happened to the engineer."

Jen pulled out her phone and called Howell. She put him on speaker phone.

"You all make it?" Howell asked.

"Of course," Jen said. "What have you got for us?"

"I've got an engineer standing by," Howell said. "You're about ten minutes out from Kingston, so I'll conference him in. Just a sec."

Jen peered out the window. Trees zipped by. Few buildings.

"Howell here. Do I still have you, Jen?"

"Yup."

"Reynolds?"

"I'm here."

"Who's going to play engineer?" Howell asked.

Zeke jumped up and down with his hand up. "Me. Me."

Jen and Wayne exchanged amused glances. "Zeke will stop the train."

"Give Zeke the phone," Howell said. "Take it off speaker so it'll be easier to hear. We don't want any mistakes on this."

Jen handed Zeke the phone and he glided to the controls, nodding his head and speaking into the phone.

"What's the Kingston area like?" Jen asked.

Wayne rubbed his nose. "A few roads and lots of trees, but the University of Rhode Island is nearby, so there could be a lot of people in the crosshairs."

"Sounds like a shitty tactical plan," D-Day said.

Jen put an arm around the gruff biker. "Thanks for the helping hand back there."

He didn't push her hand away or make a fuss, but his cheeks reddened.

"What branch of the military did you serve in?" Wayne asked.

D-Day's expression froze. "Army."

"My friend Mark was in the Army, too," Jen said. "Flew helicopters, then got screwed over by an officer and ended up doing convoys. Said he spent a lot of time waiting for an IED to explode underneath him."

One of D-Days eyebrows rose. "Convoys are the second craziest things to do."

"What's the craziest?" Jen asked.

"What I did. EOD."

"Defusing bombs?" Wayne asked.

"Yup. Convoys spent their time trying to avoid the explosives. We spent our time getting to know them. You can't do that job if you're sporting a full deck."

Zeke joined them, the phone still to his ear. "Brace yourselves. We're about to stop."

Jen found a corner and slid to the floor. She braced her feet against a console.

Wayne sat next to her and D-Day stayed on his feet, watching out the window.

The train slowed. Not much, but it definitely slowed. Zeke had the phone glued to his ear and he worked the console. The train's speed dropped until it was barely chugging along.

Zeke looked back. "Hang on."

The brakes were applied and Jen resisted the pull forward. Loud squealing and hydraulic sounds came from outside and the train slowed to a stop.

"I did it," Zeke yelled.

Jen took the phone from him and switched it back to speaker. "Howell, you there?"

"Haven't left. Everyone OK?"

"Of course, but I'm beginning to wonder if there's anything Zeke can't do."

Zeke grinned. "I've done it before. I had the best train simulator on my computer back home."

"What about the state troopers?" Jen asked. "Are they in position?"

"Checked with them minutes ago," Howell said. "They're ready. They've taken up position in the terminal."

D-Day grunted. "Guess it's time to get the show on the road. How about opening the car doors, Zeke?"

Zeke hurried to the console and pushed a button. "Done deal."

"Which one did you open?" Howell asked.

"Which one?" Zeke repeated. "All of them."

"Shit," Howell said. "There are ten cars and each carries sixty-two people. That's a ton to set loose all at once. I expected you to open them one at a time and let the troopers mop them up before you opened another."

Growling came from outside. Jen stuck her head out and looked back at the cars. She pulled her head back in. "They're pouring out of the cars."

"Close the damn door," D-Day said.

Jen pulled to slide it closed, but it didn't budge. D-Day and Wayne joined her, the three of them grunting and straining, but the door was frozen open.

"Find something to hide behind," Jen said. "And stay quiet."

The console that sat in the middle of the floor provided the best coverage, and Jen joined D-Day and Wayne there. Zeke squeezed between two consoles on the other side. *He's the only one skinny enough to fit.*

The zombies approached and the gunshots started. Jen peered around the console. Hundreds of zombies passed by. Several of them were dropped by bullets, but the rest went into a run.

Something tells me they don't have enough state troopers to take care of that.

A few minutes passed and no more zombies passed by. Jen crept to the door and peeked outside. The horde was attacking the terminal. *Looks like the troopers have their hands full.*

She stood on her tiptoes and peered out the front window. The zombies had massed and were pushing toward the terminal. *But that doesn't look like six hundred and twenty people to me.*

She turned to Zeke. "I think a bunch of them are heading into the trees."

Something ran into her back, whiplashing her neck and slamming her into a console. She fell to the floor with a heavy weight on her chest.

16

Jen's lungs emptied from the impact. She gasped for breath and choked on the graveyard fumes from the zombie.

D-Day grabbed the zombie's hair and yanked its head back before its snapping jaws could clamp onto her throat. The biker's machete cleaved the zombie's skull and it slumped.

Wayne knelt by Jen's side. "Come on. We have to go."

D-Day threw the twice-dead corpse out of the door and Zeke took up a position next to him while Wayne pulled Jen to her feet. She leaned on him and almost fell, but he wrapped an arm around her waist and kept her up.

Gunshots from the terminal increased.

"Now," D-Day yelled. "Head for the troopers."

Zeke let out a whoop and jumped out of the engine room, his katana over his head. D-Day hopped down a second later.

Wayne led Jen to the doorway. "I'll help you down."

Jen pushed him. "I can do it myself."

He grinned and climbed to the ground.

She jumped, almost losing her balance as her feet hit the gravel, but Wayne stayed back.

In full ninja mode, Zeke sliced an arm off one zombie, then spun and beheaded another. In contrast with his grace, D-Day bulled his way through the horde. He slammed the machete blade through one zombie's skull, then kicked another away before he bashed a third in the temple with the machete's handle.

More zombies fell as bullets flew from the terminal.

The terminal.

Jen pulled her tomahawk and stumbled toward the yellow building. Zeke and D-Day were keeping the front edge of the horde back and she was going to take advantage of the head start.

Coming around the front of the engine, a large woman with long steel-gray hair lurched toward her. Jen timed the zombie's movements with her own and swung sidearm, punching the pointed end of the tomahawk into the zombie's skull just behind an eye. The zombie fell against the engine and slid to the ground. *I'm getting the hang of this weapon.*

Wayne rushed to her and she let him lead her to the terminal's far side, where the troopers were positioned. They ceased firing as Jen and Wayne got closer then rushed out to help them to safety.

Jen leaned against the building, finally catching her breath. She looked up as Zeke and D-Day dashed around the corner.

"Is that everyone?" a sergeant asked.

Jen nodded. Five troopers shot into the horde. "Are there more of you?"

"On their way," the sergeant said.

"You've got to be kidding," D-Day growled.

Slipping the tomahawk back in its holster, Jen walked out from the side of the building. The horde of about fifty zombies stampeded toward them. She pulled her pistol and emptied a magazine of fourteen rounds, only killing five. *Shit. Still shaky.*

D-Day, Wayne, and Zeke joined her, and the charging horde was destroyed in minutes.

The sergeant walked over. "Thanks for the assist."

"That's not all of them," Jen said.

"What do you mean?"

D-Day nodded. "She's right. That was about one car's worth. And there are ten cars."

"They had to have gone into the woods," Zeke said.

The sergeant walked away and spoke into a radio, his face grim. He came back a minute later. "You folks need to get somewhere safe while we clear the area."

Jen scowled. "I need to get something out of the train first. Then we'll start it back up and finish the trip to Boston."

"I'm afraid that's not going to happen," the sergeant said.

Jen removed her badge from her back pocket and held it up. "I'm afraid it is."

The sergeant's jaw tightened, but he gave her a curt nod.

Jen strode toward the train. *Feeling like my old self again.*

D-Day took position on her right and Wayne lined up on her left. Zeke took the rear.

Jen stopped outside the doorway to the first car. "Zeke comes in with me and you two stand watch out here."

D-Day nodded. Wayne frowned and nodded.

Jen entered the car with her tomahawk cocked back. No sign of anyone.

Zeke crept up the aisle, and Jen followed. She checked the seats in each row, and the floor beneath them.

They reached the front of the car. "Nothing," she said. "I was sure it was here."

She strode to the door and stuck her head out. "Not here. Going to the second car."

Wayne and D-Day positioned themselves by the outside door to the second car.

Jen stepped through the doorway between the cars and walked down the aisle checking each seat. She stopped about halfway through and squinted at something on the floor at the other end of the car. *Is that what I think it is?*

"Found it." She ran to the pouch. It lay next to the doorway to the third car.

She knelt and picked it up. The strap was missing the buckle. "Sure as shit, it must've been stripped from my waist during all the action."

Pulling the zipper open, she looked back at Zeke walking toward her with one of his big goofy smiles. His jaw dropped and his eyes threatened to pop out of his head. "Jen." He sprinted toward her.

Hot coals burned into her forearm. She jerked her head around. A chunk of flesh and muscle had been ripped away, the grotesque wound wet and bloody. The edges of the wound turned black and spread up her arm as she watched.

A legless zombie lay on the floor chewing its prize.

Jen scrambled backward, then lost her balance and slammed to the floor. Zeke dashed past her. "No," he screamed.

His katana flashed and removed the zombie's head in one stroke. He knelt next to Jen, holding her wounded arm. "I'm sorry. I'm so sorry. I was supposed to protect you."

D-Day and Wayne rushed in and came to a stop, their eyes telling Jen what they were thinking.

"You have to kill me," she said.

Wayne looked away. D-Day's eyes grew cold and steely. *He's working himself up to it.*

A burning shock of pain exploded throughout her body and she screamed, her back arching. "The poison's moving fast. Do it now. I don't want to hurt any of you."

Zeke turned away for a moment, then back. He held a hypodermic needle.

Another flood of fire traced down Jen's spine. She gasped. Unable to speak, she shook her head at Zeke. *Don't waste it.*

Tears streaming from his red-rimmed eyes, Zeke plunged the needle into Jen's undamaged arm and depressed the plunger.

The serum entered her veins as cold as glacier water. The fire in the other arm had reached her shoulder. The icy serum shot up her vein and into her heart just as the poison reached the beating organ.

Jen screamed as they collided. Her heart seized and her body convulsed. Searing pain covered every inch of her body and the smell of dead flesh invaded her mind.

I'm turning.

17

Jen floated in pitch black nothingness. No sense of sight, sound, or touch. *Am I dead?*

A voice in her head answered. "No. You are with us."

So I'm alive? Who are you? Where am I?

"You are neither dead or alive."

Fuck you. I'm not a zombie. My friends would've kept me from that.

"True. You're also not undead. You are a fascinating bridge between us and living humans."

Where am I?

"In our group consciousness."

What is that? And who the hell are you?

"Time for you to awaken and discover your fate."

WHO ARE YOU?

"You know the answer to that. I was so sad to see you fly away from Fairchild just as I and my troops arrived."

Jen's eyes slitted open. Blurry figures leaned over her. They were saying something, but it sounded like gibberish.

Her brain was on fire and her heart beat impossibly fast. A picture formed in her mind. She stood before the pit and the sailors rose, their arms outstretched toward her. She tried to flee, but her legs froze to the spot.

The overwhelming grave stench washed over her as the zombies gathered around her, then dropped to their knees and bent their heads as if they were knights kneeling before their queen.

She raised a hand to rub her eyes, hoping she'd wake up. She stopped, her hand in front of her face. The flesh had rotted, and hung in shreds. Glistening white bones shone through.

The voice came back. "You are one of us now."

Jen screamed.

Visions came and went, from a fiery pit of molten rock she tried to escape from to iceberg-laden water she was drowning in. *No more pain. Please!*

"Jen."

She kept her eyes closed. Was this just another dream?

Closer, the voice said, "Jen, can you hear me?"

I know that voice.

She murmured, "Wayne?"

Wayne laughed. "Yeah, it's me. Can you open your eyes?"

Her eyelids were stuck together, but she strained and they popped open. A face hovered above her, blurry. "Wayne."

The blurry face shot away and someone nearby took in a lungful of air.

"Wayne?" she asked.

Wayne's voice came, but this time it was shaky. "How do you feel?"

Jen blinked several times and his face came into focus. She smiled. "For once, I'm glad you asked. It was pretty shitty for a while, but I think I'm over the fever."

She rose on her elbows and Wayne scooted back. "What the hell's wrong with you?" she asked.

He swallowed, his Adam's apple bobbing on his neck. "You were bitten."

Jen raised the arm that had been bitten. It was wrapped in bandages and blood had seeped through and dried. She flexed it. "Doesn't hurt."

Zeke had given her the serum. "So the serum worked?" She looked around the room. A small office with two desks and two chairs, it smelled of grease and oil. She lay on a couch with a cheap plastic cover.

"Where am I?"

"My shop," Wayne said. "In Coventry, Rhode Island. D-Day found a couple of motorcycles. One had a sidecar, and we put you in it and rode here as fast as we could."

"Where are the others? Where's Zeke? I need to thank him."

Wayne glanced at a closed door. "They're in the shop."

Jen pushed herself into a sitting position and shook her head. "Still some cobwebs. How long was I out?"

"A day."

Damn.

She pointed to a door on the opposite wall. "Bathroom?"

Wayne nodded.

Jen pushed herself to her feet and used a desk as

support as she stumbled toward the bathroom. Wayne backed up to the shop door. His hand gripped the knob as if he were about to make a run for it.

Jen ignored him and made it to the bathroom. Hanging onto the doorframe with one hand, she fumbled along the wall for a switch. She found it after a moment and flipped it on.

Sharp fluorescent light blinded her. She rubbed her eyes with the heels of her hands, then opened them.

The small bathroom had a standard toilet with a seat that had seen better times. The floor tiles were worn, but clean, and a sink with a rust stain down the back of the basin stood directly in front of her. A mirror hung on the wall above it.

She glanced in the mirror, then did a double-take. A worn version of herself, with torn dirty clothes and disheveled black hair, stared back at her.

A chill hit her body and she trembled. One brown eye peered back at her. Only one, because the other was deep yellow.

18

Jen froze. "Holy shit."

She spun. "You need to kill me now. Before I finish turning and hurt you."

Wayne put his hands out, shaking his head. "No. You were bitten yesterday."

A bang came at the door. "I hear you talking," Zeke said. "Is she awake?"

Jen looked at herself in the mirror again. "I can't let anyone see me like this. Especially not Zeke."

The door burst open and D-Day strode in, shoving it to the side. "How is she?"

Jen shut her eyes.

Someone hugged her from behind. "You don't know how glad I am to see you alive," Zeke said.

Keeping her eyes shut, Jen turned and hugged him back. "Not sure I am."

Zeke let go of her.

"What do you mean?" D-Day rumbled.

Jen took a deep breath and exhaled. She opened her eyes.

D-Day's jaw went slack and he yanked his machete from its sheath.

Zeke's mouth formed a perfect "O," then broke into a smile that threatened to cut his face in half. "Gnarly."

He took a step toward her and she put her hands out. "No. We don't know if I'm dangerous."

D-Day remained silent, his eyes boring into hers as if trying to read her mind.

"I think she's OK," Wayne said. "She would've turned completely a long time ago."

"Come on," Zeke said. "You're the same Jen we all know and love. You just have the coolest eyes I've ever seen."

Jen lumbered to the couch and dropped onto it. "But we don't know if it's over. Remember that experiment with the old lady that gave O'Connor the heart attack? The serum delayed her turning."

"But not by a day," Zeke said.

"And now we don't have the serum," Jen said. "Our mission was to deliver it so it could be used to make a cure for everyone, not just me."

Zeke stood back, arms crossed. "I had to save you. I had no choice."

D-Day still had the machete in his hand.

Jen's eyes met his. "You can do it. We haven't known each other long."

"Oh, I'll do it," D-Day said. "But only if the time comes. I'm not a murderer."

Jen squeezed her eyes shut and leaned back on the couch. "My mission's changed. Since we no longer have the serum, we need to go back to Atlanta."

"That's the first sensible thing you've said since you woke up," D-Day said. "I'll take you in the sidecar, but we need to find a place to fill up."

"I've got an underground tank here," Wayne said. "You're welcome to it."

"Where Jen goes, I go," Zeke said.

Wayne exhaled loudly. "I knew you'd say that. Looks like Zeke and I are coming along."

D-Day rubbed his hands together. "Now that's settled, where can we get some grub?"

Wayne pointed toward the front glass door. "Burger place on the opposite corner of the intersection and a greasy spoon across the street to the left."

"Burgers it is." D-Day opened the door.

"Wait," Jen said. "I can't go out there like this."

Wayne frowned, then yanked a desk drawer open and rustled through it, finally producing a black pair of sunglasses.

He handed them to Jen. "This should do."

She put them on and looked in the mirror. "Close up, I can tell my eyes are different colors, but not that one is yellow."

"They'll do for now," D-Day said. "We'll pick up some mirror sunglasses after we eat."

Jen nodded. "I'm hungry, too."

She followed D-Day out the door and to the burger place. Zeke kept pace by her side. Wayne stopped and locked the shop's door before joining them.

Feeling better. Bet some food will take me to a hundred percent.

The restaurant had a few people in it. D-Day led them to a table in the back. Seventies' classic rock music played over speakers that looked like they'd seen better days.

A large sign hung on the wall that said, "Clam Cakes and Chowda Our Specialty."

A grimy-looking guy with a unibrow took their order. Jen chose a double cheeseburger.

"How would you like that cooked?" Grimy Guy asked.

"Raw."

D-Day and Wayne did a double take, and Zeke's mouth hung open. Grimy Guy looked at her, the furry caterpillar over his brow crinkled. "You mean rare?"

She glanced at the others, then grinned. "Let's make it well done."

Wayne visibly relaxed, while Zeke's mouth shut. D-Day went back to his complacent-looking expression. "Looks like you haven't changed that much," he grumbled.

Jen wolfed down her food, then sat back and finished her soda. A light belch escaped. "Feel like my old self again."

"You look like a celebrity with sunglasses on indoors," Zeke said.

Wayne laughed.

"I make these look cool," Jen replied.

Jen's fingertips tingled.

What was that?

Jen glanced toward the back wall. Nothing but booths and wall.

The tingling traveled up her arm and snaked down her spine. She turned her chair toward the wall. *Something's wrong.*

D-Day finished off a large shake, then put a hand up.

The music on the radio had stopped and it emitted a series of beeps. "This is the emergency broadcast system. Stand by for an important message from the Rhode Island Department of Emergency Management."

Someone at another table gave a loud *shhh* and the burger joint went quiet.

"There has been a zombie outbreak in Kingston," the

radio said. "While that outbreak was resolved, Rhode Island state troopers report that breakouts have occurred in North Kingstown, Exeter, East Greenwich, Warwick, and West Warwick. Citizens in those areas are cautioned to arm themselves and stay in their homes or places of employment. Call 911 to report any zombie activity."

A couple of cop cars zoomed by with their sirens screaming. They were followed by SUVs full of men in camouflage uniforms, heading in the same direction Jen had just been sensing something.

"What's out in that direction?" D-Day asked.

"West Warwick," Wayne said. "Just down the road."

Chairs scraped the floor as the other table of diners hurriedly left.

"I want to go see," Jen said. *I have to go see.*

"Are you nuts?" Wayne said. "Why do you want to do that?"

Jen looked at D-Day. A small grin appeared on his face. *Damn, he always looks like he knows more of what's going on than everyone else.*

Zeke stood. "Because that's what we do, Wayne. We're Homeland Security agents, and we kill zombies."

"And there's no serum left to guard," Jen said. "Why not help out the locals before we return to Atlanta?"

"Damn straight." D-Day stood and headed for the door.

Jen shoved the last French fry into her mouth and rushed after him.

The two bikes roared down Tiogue Ave until it became Main Street. Several cars passed them going the other way. *Guess it's worth your rations to get the hell out of Dodge when the undead show up.*

The sidecar hit a pothole and Jen was thrown against the back. "Dammit. Rhode Island roads suck."

Lined with older-looking two-story houses, the area looked like it probably hadn't changed in fifty years.

Several pickups rode up on their ass and laid on their horns. D-Day and Wayne moved to the side to let them pass. Filled with men and women in a mishmash of camouflage and denim clothing, each wielding a variety of weapons, they sped by and disappeared up ahead.

The cracked sidewalks filled with pedestrians heading away from the action. Some carried possessions, but most had nothing more than the clothes on their back. A number of bicycles sped by on the road.

Two minutes later, they came to a number of vehicles blocking the road between a pharmacy and a two-story brick building. Police vehicles with their lights still going were parked next to civilian vehicles, including the trucks that had whizzed past them.

D-Day brought the bike to a stop several yards away on the grass outside the pharmacy. Wayne pulled up beside him.

The tingling had intensified and covered one whole side of Jen's body. The side she'd been bitten on. She rubbed her unaffected hand over the tingling arm and paused at the scar from the zombie bite. *What the hell is going on?*

Two armed men approached. "We've got an outbreak up ahead. Zombies everywhere. You folks need to turn around and leave."

Jen laughed. "Zombie is my middle name."

19

Jen held her badge up. "Homeland Security. Agent Reed."

One of the men stepped forward and took the badge from her. He returned to his partner and they examined the badge and whispered between themselves. The man who took the badge looked up. "And these others?"

Jen pointed to Zeke. "Agent Tripp. These other men are with us."

The man with the badge tossed it to her. "You need to check in with the chief." He led her to a West Warwick cop giving orders to a group of men.

"You guys get on the right flank and hold them," he said. "We've got to keep them from spreading out of Arctic."

He turned to Jen as she approached him. One of the men who'd challenged her team whispered in the cop's ear.

The cop smiled and thrust out a hand. "Agent Reed? I'm Captain Leander. I'm in charge here."

Jen shook his hand, then pointed at Zeke and the others in turn. "Agent Tripp, his brother, Wayne, and D-Day."

Leander shook each of their hands, but gave D-Day an extra once-over. "What can I do for you?"

"What's your sitrep?" D-Day asked.

Leander looked from D-Day to Jen. She shrugged. "Good question."

He pointed to their left. "Outbreak started at the senior center and—"

Jen's tingling went into overdrive just as a twenty-something zombie with stringy, blood-matted hair stumbled from around the corner of the pharmacy.

Jen put up a hand. "Don't shoot."

With a puzzled expression, Leander waved his hand. "Hold fire."

The zombie was missing a chunk of meat from its left thigh, but it continued to limp toward Jen. She pulled her tomahawk and strode toward the zombie.

Someone behind her murmured, "What the hell's she doing?"

A sharp *shh* quieted him.

Jen's tingling became stronger, painful, as if a thousand needles were being jammed into the bitten side of her body.

The zombie's head tilted back and the hair covering the face fell away.

Jen winced and gritted her teeth. *Got to ignore the pain.*

She charged the zombie with the tomahawk cocked over her head. Swinging it down, she slammed the blade into the zombie's forehead, holding back enough to just wound it.

Facing the cops and militia, she held up a hand to stop a militia woman who was raising her shotgun. Leander shot the woman a glare and she lowered her weapon.

The zombie stopped and shuffled, turning to face Jen. She pressed her bitten arm to her side and gasped as a bolt of electricity shot up her side. *Got to take this thing out now. Enough experimenting.*

She stepped into her strike, bringing the pointed end of the tomahawk around and punching it into the zombie's right eye. It dropped to the ground, the goo from the punctured eye dripping from the tomahawk.

The pain, the electricity down Jen's side vanished. Jen panted. *That's some interesting shit.*

She walked back to the others. "Chief," she said, "we're going in."

"Do what you want," Leander said. "We're still waiting for more men before we push in, so we won't be able to help you if you run into trouble."

Jen grinned. *Who the hell in this world has been in more zombie trouble than me?* "Understood."

She moved several yards back from Leander and his people. Wayne, D-Day, and Zeke gathered around her.

"I want you guys to know what's going on. No secrets." She paused and looked at each in turn. Wayne had a look of concern, while D-Day's perma-frown didn't waver. Zeke couldn't keep still, moving his weight back and forth between his legs. *He's like an ADD sixth grader.*

"You wondered what the bite and serum might have done to me, besides the trendy two-toned eyes." She took a deep breath. "I can feel when a zombie is close by."

"What does that mean?" D-Day asked. "Feel?"

"I can't explain it very well, at least not yet. But I felt it all the way back at the diner. It got stronger as we got closer to this spot." None of their expressions changed.

"Look," she said, "when that zombie showed itself, the feeling shot through me like an electric shock. It hurt like hell, and it didn't stop until I killed it."

"Do you feel any other zombies around now?" Wayne asked.

She shrugged. "I have the low-level uneasiness I first felt at the diner. But the pain and high intensity sensations turned off like someone had flipped a switch."

"You get the most awesome stuff," Zeke said.

Jen rolled her eyes at him. "We'll see how awesome it is."

"And that's why you want to go in," D-Day said. "See if it happens again. Experiment."

"Bingo."

He slipped the machete from its sheath. "Let's do it."

"We've got our own zombie detector," Zeke said.

Leander walked over. "When are you going in? I've got my men positioned and we can cover you."

"Right now," Jen said. "Where are the cleared areas?"

He pointed to the left of the intersection. "Anything that way. All cleared."

Jen positioned herself out in front of the vehicles and the troops taking cover behind them. Sensations came from a one-hundred-degree radius up the street. *They're all over in that direction.*

She pointed to a bank. "We'll head there and start clearing out buildings."

D-Day took a step forward, but Jen put an arm out and he stopped. He glanced at her arm and then at her as if to say her puny arm could do nothing to stop him.

"Better let me go first," she said. "With this new sense, I might be able to detect a horde or an ambush quicker."

"Makes sense." He stepped aside.

Jen peered down the road to her right. It looked abandoned, the only thing moving was a sheet of newspaper blowing down the sidewalk.

Zeke stood next to her. "Where are they?"

Tingling ran up Jen's side. "They're out there."

She approached the bank's glass door, trying to peer inside for any movement. D-Day took up position on one side of the door, while Wayne took the other. "Zeke and I will go in first," she said.

Wayne pulled the door open and held it. Walking on the balls of her feet, Jen choked up on the tomahawk and crept in. Zeke had his katana held ready, and he entered by her side.

It was a small bank, and Jen could see most of it from the door. Nothing stirred, so she gestured for Zeke to approach the teller windows on the right while she took the left. She got up on her tiptoes to look over the counter. There was nothing but empty stools and papers scattered across the floor.

Wayne entered the building and crept toward the single restroom door. D-Day hustled to catch up with him. "Don't go wandering off alone."

D-Day pushed the door open, revealing a lightless room of shadows. Wayne reached in and flipped the switch. D-Day let the door close. "Nothing."

The tingling had dropped to almost nothing. It was like playing the kid's game Hot and Cold. The tingling increased when she was near a zombie, and died when they were far enough away. *I wonder if having buildings and walls between me and the zombies makes a difference?*

She walked toward the back door, which had an exit sign above it. The tingling slowly built back up. "This way."

The door opened into a back parking lot with an ATM drive. Older homes sat across the road.

Jen took several steps into the parking lot and looked down the street. *Still nothing.*

Zeke hitched his thumb to the right. "Do you want us to

do this building next? If I don't get to kick some zombie ass soon, I'm going to burst."

The next building over was the back entrance to a store. A two-story white building with fresh colorful paint, it stood in sharp contrast to the bank with its barred windows and plain exterior.

Jen approached the store and stopped, clenching her teeth. The tingling down her side went into overdrive. "They're close. Be ready."

Wayne put a hand to his ear. "Listen."

The sound of hundreds of pounding feet came from down the road.

"Get in the building," Jen yelled.

20

Jen dashed through the doors, nearly running over Zeke, who stood looking at the oncoming horde with a faint smile on his face. She grabbed him by the sleeve and pulled him inside.

D-Day and Wayne pulled the doors closed and followed Jen and Zeke into the small shop. She led them to the far side of the store where a staircase went to the second floor. No sooner had they reached the stairs than banging began at the back doors.

D-Day pointed at the store's front windows, which looked out over Main Street. Scores of zombies raced past, heading for the militia lines. Guns barked and men yelled as they engaged the horde.

"We're surrounded," Wayne said. "Can't go out the front or back."

"Then we go up." Jen climbed the stairs, which opened onto a landing with three closed doors. Jen opened the one straight ahead and turned on the light. A small office, it had an industrial metal desk, a reclining chair patched with electrical tape, and a cabinet overflowing with papers.

"Nothing in here." She closed the door and turned to the others. D-Day had opened one door and Zeke the other. He immediately closed his, holding his nose. "Just the bathroom."

D-Day stepped through the third door and disappeared for a moment. He stuck his head back out. "Looks like this is our best bet."

Jen followed Wayne inside. "An apartment?"

"A lot of these buildings that have businesses on the first floor have apartments on the second," Wayne said.

The banging downstairs increased. Jen crept to the top of the stairway. The left side of her body had gone practically numb from her built-in zombie detection alarm. *There has to be more of them.*

"I don't think we have more than five minutes before they're inside." She peered down the stairway trying to see the shadow-covered stairs. She flipped a switch on the wall and an overhead light buzzed, flickered, and went dark. "Shit."

She took her sunglasses off and put them in her shirt pocket. *Better.*

Wayne stood in the apartment doorway. "Come on."

She turned to him and he flinched. She almost felt like apologizing. *I wonder if any of them will ever look at me the same again.*

"I'm staying here," Jen said. "Top of the stairs is a good choke point."

Zeke pushed past Wayne. "Then I'm standing there with you."

Jen shook her head. "Narrow stairs. Only room for one. You should take that doorway to the apartment as a choke point. Keep the door closed. The three of you can defend it once it's breached."

D-Day tromped toward her. "Bullshit. We don't need heroes."

Jen smiled. "Looks like you're getting all emotional on me, big guy. Who said I was going to let myself get overrun? I'll hold this choke point until I can't hold it anymore, then I'm falling back into the apartment with you. I'll catch my breath while the three of you defend the door. That is, if you can handle it for a few minutes without me."

D-Day clenched his fists and lumbered back into the apartment. "Damn Homeland Security agents," he murmured.

Wayne followed him in, but Zeke didn't move. "You got bit because of me and I don't feel right leaving you out here to get bit again."

Jen's left leg spasmed. "The freaking zombies will be in here in another minute. I need you back in the apartment, and I won't take your shit. I've already been bitten and haven't turned, so I'm probably immune. That's more than I can say for you."

Zeke stared at her for a moment, then said, "I'll leave. But if I think you aren't coming back, I'm coming out to get you."

Jen grinned. "I expect nothing less. Now get the hell out of here."

Zeke disappeared and the door closed. The gunfire and the banging had reached a crescendo. *Sounds like they're hammering in the front door, too.*

Jen positioned herself two steps down the stairway and took a couple practice swings with the tomahawk. *I should be able to hold this thing for a while.*

A crash and the tinkle of shattering glass came from downstairs. Banging, as if furniture was being tossed aside followed, and underneath it all, the shuffling of dozens of feet.

A wave of zombies flooded the bottom of the stairwell, creating a pile of intertwined limbs and snarling, yellow-eyed faces. Blood poured from their wounds and predator eyes searched for prey.

Jen widened her stance and bent her knees slightly, swinging the tomahawk back and forth. Two zombies broke from the pileup and raced up the stairs toward her. Twenty steps, fifteen, ten.

The lead zombie's eyes burned into hers, but it stopped two steps away. Its head tilted as its gaze bore into hers. "One more step and I'm dropping your ass," she said.

The second zombie clambered to get over the first, but stopped as his eyes locked with Jen's.

What the hell? They look confused.

"You can't tell if I'm friend or foe, can you?"

She closed her human eye. Both zombies straightened and stumbled down the stairs. The pile of zombies at the bottom unraveled and headed into the store.

"Well I'll be dipped in dogshit."

Jen crept down the stairs and peeked out. The zombies poured out the front door and joined the street zombies attacking the militia.

Jen opened her human eye.

Boots stomped down the stairs behind her and Jen spun, bringing her tomahawk above her head.

Wayne and Zeke stood at the bottom of the stairwell, their weapons raised with puzzled looks on their faces. D-Day clomped down and leaned on the railing. "I guess you didn't need our help," he said.

Jen shrugged. "When you've got it, you've got it."

The horde on Main Street surged past, their attention on the militia.

Wayne stood next to Jen, watching them flow past. His

hand brushed hers. Jen's heartbeat picked up. *We're going to have to do something about this when the time is right.*

She swallowed and turned to him. "Sorry I didn't leave you any."

He gave her his crooked grin. "That's okay. Looks like there's plenty more." His eyebrows lowered. "But what happened? We didn't hear any fighting and there are no bodies."

D-Day lumbered forward. "That's a question I'd like answered, too. What the hell's going on?"

Jen licked her lips. "They didn't attack me at first, I think because of my yellow eye. But they were thinking about it. So I closed my human eye, leaving only the yellow open, and they turned around and walked away."

"Holy shit," Wayne said. "They thought you were one of them."

D-Day didn't say anything, just stood there with his arms crossed and his eyes staring beneath bushy brows.

"Damn, Jen," Zeke said. "Someone's going to have to write a comic book about you." He laughed. "Zombie fighter Jen and her sidekick, Zeke the ninja." He took a couple of swipes with his katana.

D-Day went to the back door. "Totally busted back here. The front doors will keep out any strays but it's open season from the rear. We should move."

"What about the militia?" Jen said.

D-Day shook his head. "I ain't afraid of a fight, but attacking that mob out there would be suicide."

"He's right," Wayne said. "The militia was expecting reinforcements, and they'll do them a lot more good than we will. Besides, I think we need to find out more about your new...condition, and what you can do with it."

Jen sighed. "Agreed. We should probably move to the next—"

A sharp pain in her gut folded her in half. Wayne grabbed her and kept her from falling. "What's wrong?"

D-Day and Zeke rushed over.

"Don't know," Jen grunted. The pain subsided enough for her to straighten, but it was still strong and getting stronger.

She looked out the front window. The horde had passed, but one figure walked unsteadily toward the front door. An older lady, her skin hanging loose on her bony frame, shuffled to the door and peered in, her yellow gaze sweeping the room and resting on Jen. She reached out and pulled the door open. *A leader.*

Zeke stepped forward, his katana ready to attack. "What are you doing?"

Jen put her arms out, her gut still twisting. "Step back. Don't attack unless she does first."

Jen waited as the old lady shuffled to her. The zombie stopped and examined her from head to foot then stared into her eyes. A buzzing grew in Jen's head and the pain disappeared. Not unpleasant, the buzzing grew louder.

"You guys hear anything?" she asked.

"Not me," Zeke said.

"Nope," D-Day said.

"You're the only one," Wayne added. "What are you hearing?"

The buzzing reached a crescendo, then stopped. The feeling of being under a microscope rushed over her. "Do you understand me?" Jen asked.

The zombie continued to stare, motionless.

Jen took a deep breath and exhaled. "If you understand me, raise your right hand."

The zombie's right arm jerked up. Jen gasped. "Lower your arm." The arm dropped.

"Do you know who I am?" The zombie's right arm shot up. Jen's heart hammered her chest.

"Am I talking to the old lady who stands before me?" The zombie didn't move.

"If the answer is no, please raise your left hand." The zombie's left hand lifted.

Jen's breathing became shallow and rapid. She stumbled and Wayne rushed forward, putting his arm around her waist. She leaned against him.

"Jen?" he said.

She ignored him and locked eyes with the zombie. *Let's get to the nitty-gritty.*

Forcing the words from her mouth, Jen asked, "Am I talking to Butler?"

The zombie's right arm shot up.

21

Zeke jumped in front of Jen and knocked the old lady to the floor. She sprung at him as soon as she landed.

Zeke spun, the katana a blur.

"No," Jen cried.

The zombie collapsed at Zeke's feet and its head flew, striking Wayne's chest and bouncing onto the floor. Wayne scrambled backward, brushing his shirt. "Shit!"

Jen grabbed Zeke by the collar. "What'd you do that for?"

Zeke's eyes were downcast. "It was Butler. You said he needs to die."

"I wanted to find out more from him. I need to know why he keeps trying to contact me." Zeke wouldn't meet her gaze. *He did what he's always doing—protecting me.*

She released her grip and straightened his collar. "Sorry about the reaction."

A goofy grin spread across his face. "No worries."

"What do you mean when you say he keeps trying to contact you?" D-Day asked.

Jen licked her lips. Zeke and Wayne moved closer.

"The drones in the CDC basement," she said. "I think Butler could see through them, but he didn't have as much control."

Wayne rubbed his chin. "But he has clearer communication with leaders?"

Jen nodded. "I think so. First it was O'Connor and now this old lady. You saw what happened."

Wayne pointed out the front window. "Look."

The disciplined army of zombies had turned into an unorganized mob, but still pushed up the street in the direction of the gunshots.

"That leader must've been directing the drones," Zeke said. "Now they're just a normal, everyday horde."

D-Day lumbered to the back door. "Then now's the time to leave."

"Agreed." Jen followed him and stuck her head out of the door. "It's clear."

She crept into the parking lot and scanned the area. *Butler knows where I am. He'll find himself another leader sooner or later and have the whole horde rain down on our heads.*

Jen sprinted to the side of the next building and peered around it. The street was deserted. D-Day pushed up against her. "What do you see?"

"Nothing." She slinked out from cover. The small one-story building housed a jewelry store. "Nice bars on the window, but can't see shit from there."

Approaching the building, she craned her neck to get a good look at what lay ahead. Her zombie side went numb. *Looks like my spidey senses are tingling again.* The barred glass door of the jewelry store slammed open and an older man with balding gray hair, a huge beer belly, and organs hanging from a gash in his side lumbered forward.

D-Day swung his barrel toward the zombie, Zeke took an attack stance, and Wayne choked up on his bat.

The zombie stumbled past Jen. She put a hand up and gestured for the others to get back. The zombie seemed locked in on Wayne.

Jen ran in front of the zombie, blocking it. It stopped and glared, then shuffled around her.

She jumped in front of it again. "Stop."

Again, it went around her. *Even with my human eye showing?*

"Can I kill it now?" Zeke asked.

Jen grabbed the zombie and her body convulsed, slamming her to the ground. Her ears buzzed and everything grew darker. The last thing she saw before slipping into unconsciousness was Zeke's worried face hovering over her.

22

The buzzing grew louder until it reached a crescendo and became the whispering of a thousand voices. Blackness enveloped Jen—blackness so thick that not even a glint of light appeared.

What the hell? Am I dead?

She tried to stretch out her arms and realized she couldn't feel them. *Shit. I am dead.*

The whispering faded and a pinpoint of light appeared far away, but it grew as it came toward her. *Or am I going toward it?*

The circle of light sped toward her, filling her view then enveloping her in a blinding flash.

White. Searing white. Then it cooled and shadows appeared, becoming more distinct, until Jen found herself in a conference room, with six of the twelve chairs surrounding the table occupied.

Jen tried to move her head, look at the people around the table, but nothing she did worked. *Like watching a movie.*

A chubby thirty-something man with a shock of red hair adjusted his round wire-framed glasses and leaned forward.

"I believe the risks of Project Svengali are unacceptable." He sniffed. "And all the rewards appear to be military." He looked at Jen. "No offense, of course."

The door opened and two more people took their seats. One of them sat to her right. Her view panned to him. *O'Connor.*

Her gaze switched to the other newcomer. *Dr. Preston. And where the hell's her wheelchair?*

The redheaded man sighed. "And where's our fearless leader? Isn't our time important, too?"

The door opened and in strode Dr. Cartwright. "Forgive my tardiness. My call with the president went over its allotted time."

She sat at the head of the table and scanned the room. "Dr. Morgan. Where is he?"

Her eyes zeroed in on Jen. A voice rumbled, surrounding her like a theater sound system. "He's in the middle of a necessary procedure and will join us as soon as he can."

Cartwright stared at Jen, a tic on her eyelid the only thing giving away her thoughts. "Very well," she said. "We shall proceed."

She nodded at a stick-figure-thin woman to Jen's right. "Williams, I've read your report. Please summarize for those present."

Williams bit her lip and shuffled a stack of papers in front of her before picking up a few. "We believe we may have found viable hosts."

She looked nervously at the others and continued. "We scoured our electronic systems for any possible matches. When we found nothing substantial, we were given access to all other government agencies and expanded the search." She pushed her black plastic glasses up her nose. "Still nothing."

"Get to the point," Cartwright said.

Williams licked her lips. "We sent teams to government archive sites to go through physical documents that were never digitized. Last week, one of our teams found a promising lead in an old Navy file."

She looked down at the paper in her hands. "They assigned a naval officer, Dr. Winston Burrell, to a whaling ship in 1871 to observe and gather data on the health of the crew during the voyage. His journal is quite boring until a stopover in Haiti where he writes about a meeting with a Vodou priest, what they called a houngan."

"A witch doctor," the redheaded man interjected. "Are we here for a ghost story?"

"Quiet, Dr. Stanley," Cartwright snapped. The redheaded man sat back in his chair and said nothing.

Cartwright nodded at Williams.

"Dr. Burrell obtained a powder from the priest that he claimed had restorative properties. The doctor makes note that he tried to buy the powder but the priest refused, saying it was dangerous in the hands of anyone but a priest." She looked up. "The doctor stole the powder.

"He also notes that the priest had revealed that the person treated with the powder could be controlled by another person, but the doctor discounted that as legend.

"They sailed off the coast of Alaska, almost reaching Wainwright by August. A stationary high over Siberia reversed the normal wind pattern and pushed the pack ice toward the Alaskan coast. As we know from other historical accounts, seven of the forty ships escaped. The others were trapped in the crushing ice."

The door opened and Dr. Morgan rushed in. Taking his seat, he looked around at the others. "My apologies. Don't let me interrupt."

Williams continued, "The men became sick, and lacking the proper medication, Dr. Burrell made a tincture with the powder, dissolving it in some rum he'd obtained in the Caribbean. He gave it to the men."

Dr. Morgan leaned forward with his elbows on the table. "Here's the good part."

Williams waited. When nothing more was said, she continued. "The men got better for a time, then grew suddenly worse. The first death happened within forty-eight hours. With no place to bury him, they put the man in the hold. When the second man died hours later, they opened the hold to store him there and the first man was alive and crazed. He attacked his crewmates, ripping the flesh from their bodies and consuming it."

"Zombies?" Stanley said. "Are you serious? Maybe if you'd gone to a higher-level institution for your studies, you wouldn't be talking about ridiculous things."

Williams shrank into her seat.

Morgan clasped his hands and laid them on the table. "She's merely giving you what was written in the reports of the time."

"Fortunately," Stanley said, "we're far more sophisticated today."

What an ass.

"Let her finish." Cartwright nodded at Williams. "Let's wrap it up quickly, shall we?"

Williams took a deep breath and exhaled. She put the paper down and looked at the others as she spoke. "Dr. Burrell reported them as zombies. His last journal entry revealed that he was the only crew member who hadn't been infected. Other written Navy records reveal that those crew members walked the ice to other ships, infecting their crews. They eventually made their way to the mainland, near a small village called Point Wallace, where they froze in the subzero temperatures."

"What happened to them?" the rumbling voice asked.

"The Navy and Army sent men to collect them and bury them nearby beneath the permafrost. And so they remain today."

Stanley let out a heavy sigh. "I assume the so-called zombies are the hosts."

"So the plan would be to exhume these zombies?" the rumbling voice asked. "Then what? Bring them here? Isn't that dangerous?"

"No." Cartwright leaned forward. "Once Dr. Williams discovered this information, we scoured every piece of paper we had and found one more bit of information. It seems the government brought back samples of the zombies and studied them. It wasn't until almost twenty-five years later when science had advanced enough to detect viruses that they used that technology."

"So it is a virus?" Morgan asked.

Cartwright nodded. "The samples were destroyed, but the notes indicated it was a mycovirus."

"It attaches to spores?" Stanley said. "But that only happens with viruses that attack vegetation."

"Not anymore," Cartwright said.

"And zombies help us how?" Stanley leaned back in his chair and crossed his arms.

"Our mission," the rumbling voice said, "is to create the ability to control the troops of our enemies. This will end conflicts quicker without unnecessary risk of our own troops."

"I'm well aware of that," Stanley snapped. "What the hell do zombies have to do with it?"

Dr. Morgan removed his glasses and wiped his eyes.

"Delivery mechanism." He put his glasses back on. "If we come up with a biological method of controlling the enemy, how do we deliver it?"

"Through zombies?" Stanley sneered.

"The perfect delivery method," Cartwright said. "They bite and infect others. The outbreak grows exponentially."

Stanley pursed his lips but said nothing.

Cartwright stood. "Further discussion is moot. The president has already approved."

She opened the door and turned, her gaze burning into Jen's. "Colonel Butler, draw up a plan for delivering spores to the mass grave in Alaska. They should be buried with the bodies for eighteen months, then collected. I expect the plan on my desk by the end of the day."

"Yes, ma'am," the rumbling voice said.

23

Jen opened her eyes as far as she could and was barely able to make out D-Day on his bike. The vibrations on her back told her she was in the sidecar. "D-Day," she moaned.

He didn't react.

Can't hear me?

She tried to move, but only managed to raise a pinky finger. *What the hell's happening to me? And what about that dream? Or nightmare. I was in Butler's head, for crying out loud.*

Her body spasmed and she sank back into the shadows.

ARCTIC WIND WHIPPED past Jen's face as she stood in front of a squad of uniformed men digging. She tried to scan her surroundings, but she was back in the theater chair. *Shit. Butler again?*

One of the men shoveled up a chunk of earth, then staggered back covering his mouth and nose. The wind drove the scent up Butler's nose and his breath hitched. *And I get to smell what he smells. Freaking great.*

Butler wrapped a scarf to cover his mouth and nose and edged to the opening in the ground. "Get some light on this."

A soldier aimed his flashlight and lit the scene. *Yup. That's the sailors' pit.*

Two bearded sailor faces were exposed. One of the soldiers tapped them with a shovel. "Mostly frozen, but they're thawing."

"Let's get the damn fungus planted and cover them back up," Butler said. "Morgan? Hurry up."

Morgan, bundled up so Jen could barely make out his face, trudged into view. He removed a clear tube from inside his coat. It was filled with a brownish powder.

Butler turned around. *That's the direction of the village. Can't see a damn thing in this storm. That's how they did this without the villagers knowing.*

Butler turned back to the bodies as Morgan stood. "Get them covered up before this wind blows all the spores away," Morgan said.

Three soldiers filled in the opening to the pit.

Butler brought a radio to his lips. "Svengali One to Svengali Two. Ready for pickup."

The radio squelched. "Roger. Twenty minutes out."

Butler yelled at the soldiers. "Move your asses. You've got twenty minutes to make it look like no one's been here."

"Is she going to live?"

Zeke's voice.

Jen cracked her eyes open. Zeke sat next to her, looking behind him. "It's my fault," he said. "Never should have let that thing get so close to her."

"Screw the blame game," D-Day said. "Shit happens. Get over it."

Zeke pursed his lips.

"He's right." Wayne's voice came from in front of Zeke. "We just need to concentrate on getting her back to CDC. They'll know what to do."

"Zeke," Jen breathed.

Zeke's gaze dropped to her and his face lit up. "Jen! She's awake."

D-Day's face hovered over her. "Well, Spitfire. Looks like you cheat death again."

Jen gave him a weak smile.

"How are you feeling?" Wayne came into view.

"Weak. Confused. Can't do shit."

Zeke patted her arm. "You just relax. We've got this."

D-Day smiled. "We'll be back in Atlanta in no time."

Jen struggled to keep her eyes open, but lost the battle.

BUTLER ENTERED THE LAB.

Same one O'Connor used.

Morgan looked up from his desk. "What is it, Colonel?"

Butler's head turned from side to side. "Don't know. This whole Svengali Program just doesn't make sense to me."

"How's that?"

"It's just so off the books," Butler said. "I've been involved in hush-hush projects before, but why the hell does Cartwright report directly to the president? Even the Secretary of Defense is out of the loop."

Morgan frowned. "Does it matter as long as it works for national defense?"

A feeling of regret washed over Jen. *I'm getting his feelings, too?*

"I used to think that way," Butler said. "Sacrificed a lot of good men for the mission. Was it worth it?"

Morgan glanced at Butler over his glasses then went back to his work. "Just think if it works."

"We release the spores over enemy territory," Butler said, "then within twenty-four hours we control them. Sounds too good to be true."

Morgan didn't look up. "That's the idea."

Butler scoffed. "Nothing can go wrong with that plan, can it?"

THE TRAIN SWAYED UNDER JEN. She opened her eyes all the way. *Must be getting better.*

She lay across a seat with her head on Wayne's lap. He was fast asleep leaning against the window.

I could stay like this for awhile.

She peered across the aisle to where D-Day and Zeke sat, both out cold. Zeke leaned against D-Day and had his mouth open. A strand of drool hung off the corner of his lip, then dropped onto D-Day's arm.

Jen sighed. Were Butler's memories true, or did he just project what he wanted her to experience?

She eased herself into a sitting position. Wayne snorted and curled against the window.

Their car was empty. *How the hell did they manage that?*

She yawned. "I feel pretty good." She clamped her hand over her mouth. No need to wake the others.

Watching the countryside roll by the windows, she wondered if anything would ever get back to normal.

She leaned against the window and fell asleep.

THE DOOR to Butler's office burst open and Stanley strutted

in, his fiery hair carefully coiffed and an intense look on his face.

He shoved a large envelope at Butler. "Hide this."

"What the hell are you talking about?"

Stanley pushed it at Butler again. "You don't want to know. Just hide it where no one will find it. Someone searched my office while I was out and I know they were looking for what's in the envelope. You're the only one I can trust. Take it and I'll come back for it later. I'll explain everything then."

Stanley opened the door and stuck his head out, looking up and down the hallway. Without another word he slipped into the corridor and disappeared.

Butler opened the envelope and removed several sheets of paper. Jen couldn't read them, her vision having been blurred. *Is he keeping me from finding out what's in the envelope?*

Butler returned the papers. "Son of a bitch. Even the president's in on it."

He rose and approached a six-foot cabinet in the back of the lab. Grunting, he slid it from the wall and slipped behind it.

His hand came into view and it held a penknife. Butler used it as a makeshift screwdriver to unscrew a vent cover several inches from the floor.

When he had removed the cover, he rushed to the desk and pulled a roll of duct tape from a drawer. He placed the envelope against the top of the air duct and taped it in place. Within a couple of minutes, he had replaced the vent cover and the cabinet.

He strode toward the door. "Got to let Morgan know what's going on. I'll need him if I'm going to have a chance to stop this."

JEN JERKED awake as the train slowed. She peered out the window. "Atlanta."

"Jen." Zeke stood up in the front of the car, his eyes wide and face red.

Jen raised her hand. "Hey, Zeke."

Zeke and Wayne hovered over her.

Better not talk about the memories yet. Not until I figure out what's true or not. She stretched. "Had a good nap. A little tired, but I'll live."

D-Day stood at the front of the car with his arms crossed and his eyebrows lowered. His eyes pierced hers. *The son of a bitch always looks like he can read my mind.*

The train came to a stop at a nearly empty platform. Militia and law enforcement were stationed every fifty feet.

Zeke handed Jen her sunglasses. "Better cover up."

She slid them on.

D-Day strode to the door. "Looks a lot different than the last time we were here."

Jen rose, grasping the seatback for stability. Wayne put an arm around her. "You can lean on me."

Jen let go of the seat and allowed him to keep her on her feet. She closed her eyes and his scent filled her nostrils. *If this were another time...*

The doors slid open and two militia men jumped on board, sweeping the car. As they worked their way down the aisle, an Atlanta policeman waved at Jen and the others from the platform. "Come on out, please."

Once on the platform, Jen watched a similar scene play out at each car.

The policeman, whose name tag had "Silverio" etched

on it, looked each of them over. "Where'd you come from and what's your business here?"

Zeke displayed his badge. "Homeland Security. We're reporting to the CDC."

Silverio studied the badge for a moment, then nodded at Jen. "What's wrong with her?"

"Exhausted," she said. "Not bitten. Not infected."

Silverio motioned for three militia men to join him. He motioned to Jen. "Step forward."

Zeke opened his mouth, but the militiamen brought up their weapons. Zeke stood down.

Wayne released her and Jen shuffled to Silverio. She stopped inches away and glared at him. "Hurry the hell up. We've got a shit ton to do. In case you haven't heard, there's a war going on."

Silverio scowled. "Roll up your sleeves."

Jen peeled her sleeves back and showed her arms so that the bite scar wasn't visible.

"Turn them over," Silverio said.

Jen did, and Silverio's eyebrows rose. Two of the militiamen aimed their rifles at her.

"What's that?" Silverio asked.

Jen sighed. "I'm from Alaska. Had a bear encounter a couple of years ago."

Silverio bent over, examining her arm closely. "Looks like a human bite," he said.

"It was a black bear," Jen said. "Their bites are close to a human's. If it had been a grizzly, then my arm would be gone."

I hope he knows nothing about bears and believes the shit I'm shoveling.

"Guess you're OK."

A militiaman whispered in his ear. Silverio nodded at

Jen. "Just remove your glasses so I can see your eyes and you'll be on your way."

"I have a condition where bright light triggers migraines," Jen lied.

Silverio drew his revolver. "It's not very light inside. Show me your eyes now."

The militiamen raised their weapons.

Zeke and Wayne moved to either side of her, and the presence of the burly biker towered over all of them. Mouth dry, Jen reached for her glasses. *This isn't going to end well.*

24

Jen paused.

Screw it.

She dropped her arms and pushed past Silverio. "I don't have time for this bullshit."

Silverio grabbed her arm and she spun. "Let go or lose it," she said.

The policeman loosened his grip, but kept hold of her. "I have a job to do."

"I'm a Homeland Security agent," Jen said. "I have a bigger job than some local cop, and you're getting in the way of national security."

She pulled his hand off her. "We're leaving. If you've got a problem with that then shoot us. And when you're done you might as well put a bullet in your own head before someone else does."

She knocked a militiaman back with her shoulder as she strode from the terminal. Reaching the humid air outside, she took a deep breath.

"That was freaking awesome," Zeke said.

Wayne caught up with them. "We shouldn't hang around in case those guys grow some balls."

Unlike their departure from Atlanta, the grounds and streets around the train station were orderly. Passengers waited in cordoned-off lines that snaked through the surrounding streets.

A black limo pulled up to the curb and Mark stepped out. "Anyone looking for a ride?"

Jen smiled and gave the big man a hug. "Been keeping busy?"

Mark's grin threatened to crack his face as he returned her embrace. "Not as busy as you, I hear."

Zeke and Wayne climbed into the limo. Jen put one foot in, but stopped when her gaze fell on D-Day, who stood several yards away with his arms crossed.

Jen ducked her head inside the limo. "Give me a second."

She ran to D-Day. "You're welcome to come with us. I'm sure I can talk Cartwright into giving you a job."

"No, thanks," D-Day said. "Last time I worked for the government, it didn't work out so great."

"What are you going to do?"

He shrugged. "I've got some brothers in Atlanta I can stay with for a while. It'll give me time to figure out my next steps. Maybe I'll head north again."

Jen nodded. "Thanks for everything." She threw her arms around him and he didn't resist.

"I'll be around if you need me," D-Day said. "For a couple of weeks, anyway."

"How will I find you?"

"I'll be staying in a house just south of Emory University. Get to Clifton Road and take it to Ridgeway Drive. Fourth house on the right."

Jen nodded. "I'll remember."

The limo's horn sounded. Jen faced it and put her forefinger in the air. She turned back to D-Day. "Stay out of trouble."

The big man's face broke into a fierce grin. "Shit. Me and trouble have had a lifelong friendship."

Jen jogged to the limo and climbed in.

THE LIMO DROPPED JEN, Zeke, and Wayne off in front of the CDC Headquarters building. Within a few minutes, they stood before Cartwright.

She sat behind her desk with her fingers arched, her carefully neutral face composed. "Quite a journey. And the bottom line is we have no serum to work with."

Jen opened her mouth, but Cartwright put a hand up. "But we've got Dr. Preston working on a new serum." One eyebrow rose. "And we've got you."

Damn, she's practically drooling over me. Creepy much? "Do you think there's a cure for me?"

Cartwright's head cocked to the side. "What type of symptoms are you experiencing?"

Jen removed her sunglasses. "Yellow eye disease."

Cartwright's gaze locked onto hers. She rose and walked around the desk, never taking her eyes off Jen. "Amazing. Do you see any differently from it?"

"No."

"And what other symptoms do you have?"

Jen shrugged. *I'll be damned if I tell her anything until I find out what was on those documents Butler hid.* "Nothing else."

"Hmm." Cartwright returned to her seat. "We'll do some tests while Zeke and Wayne are gone."

"Gone?" Zeke said. "Where? When?"

"I'm sending you two, along with two other agents, back

on the train to Boston. This time you'll return with Dr. Preston."

Jen bit her lower lip. *Once Zeke and Wayne leave I'll be alone, isolated.*

Zeke frowned. "Why us?"

"We're short handed," Cartwright said. "And I'm down another two agents."

Wayne shook his head. "Rodriguez and Daniels."

Cartwright nodded.

Something heavy and cold formed in Jen's gut. *I'm stuck. I can't refuse or Cartwright might suspect something.* "You guys better get going so you can get back."

Wayne gazed into her eyes.

Another place, another time, bucko. Jen swallowed.

Zeke gave her a hug. "We'll be back before you know it." He patted the katana's hilt. "There are more chances out there to kill zombies than there is in here."

Jen let go of Zeke, put her arms around Wayne's neck, and laid her head against his chest. "Get back here fast," she whispered. "I don't feel good about this."

Wayne wrapped his arms around her. "Then I shouldn't go," he whispered back.

"Something's going on and I'm getting close to what it is. If you stay, we'll be watched, and I need the space to dig around a bit."

He released her and stepped back. His gaze dropped from her eyes to her lips. Her heartbeat kicked up a notch. *Not a good time, but I don't give a shit.*

She raised her face and he eased closer. Jen closed her eyes in anticipation.

Zeke slapped Wayne on the back. "Come on. There are zombies to kill out there."

Wayne winced and let Jen go.

Damn, Zeke. It's no wonder your parents didn't have any more kids after you were born.

"Let me know if you need us and we'll be back as soon as we can," Wayne said. Jen nodded. Wayne and Zeke left the office.

Cartwright straightened her blouse. "Let's get you down to the lab." She stopped at the door. "Better put your sunglasses back on."

ONLY THREE OF the eight rooms with test subjects were occupied. *Are they running out of volunteers or does Cartwright no longer need them now that she has me?*

Cartwright opened the door into the large cavernous room and the zombies went into a frenzy. Jen hesitated, then stepped out of the hallway.

The zombies quieted.

Cartwright glanced at Jen. "Interesting."

Yeah. Interesting. Dumb-ass zombies making it worse for me.

She glared at the one closest to her, a husky guy with shoulder-length black hair matted with chunks of decayed flesh. He stared blankly at her. She met his gaze as she passed. *Why don't you at least growl?*

The zombie bared his teeth and let out a low, menacing rumble from somewhere deep inside.

What the hell? He heard me?

"He doesn't seem to like you," Cartwright said. "But you're having some kind of effect on them. No doubt about it."

The lab door opened and O'Connor's assistant, Randy, stood in the doorway. "I'm all ready for you." He blinked and looked at the zombies. "What got into them?"

"Something with Jen, and I need you to find out what it

is," Cartwright said. "I'll check in later." She headed for the exit.

Randy nodded and stepped to the side. Jen walked into the room and he followed. "Why don't you sit?" he asked as he squeezed past her and plopped into the chair in front of the desk.

Jen took the seat next to him and rolled up her sleeves. "I'm right-handed." She stuck her left arm out.

Randy wiped her arm down. "This won't hurt."

He inserted the needle and Jen gasped. "Won't hurt?" she said.

He smirked. "I was talking about me, not you."

"For a guy who owes me big-time, you've got a funny way of showing your appreciation."

"Sorry," he said. "I get awkward when I'm uncomfortable."

He finished collecting her blood and bandaged her arm. Shaking the blood-filled tubes, he headed for the door. "Our fridge down here is on the fritz. I'll have to get these to the medical ward for refrigeration. Just hang tight."

As soon as the door closed, Jen rustled through the desk. "Aha." She took a small screwdriver from the middle drawer. Although she'd never noticed the large cabinet in her previous visits, it stuck out like a sore thumb as her eyes scanned the room.

She pulled on one side, her teeth gritted and muscles straining. It moved. Not much at first, but in several seconds she'd made a gap between the cabinet and the wall that she could squeeze into.

Sweat pasting her shirt to her skin, she wriggled into the space. Although there wasn't much light, the white vent cover was visible, just as she'd seen in Butler's memory. She soon had the cover off. She peered in, but it was too dark to make anything out, so she stuck her hand in and fumbled along the top of the vent. She touched paper.

Coughing from the dust, she ripped the envelope from its mooring and slid out from behind the cabinet and into the light.

The brown manila envelope had been opened, just as Butler had shown her. *But now I get to read it.*

She brought it to the desk and pulled the papers from it. The first page had the words *Top Secret* stamped in red, then it had a bunch of numbers to the left and a date of two years before.

Jen's eyes went to the text beneath it.

Dr. Linda Cartwright is assigned as the project lead for Project Svengali effective immediately. She will report directly to the Office of the President of the United States. All possible assistance and courtesy will be provided to her by all federal agencies.

Jen's gaze went to the big, bold signature at the bottom. *The president.*

She slid the paper to the side. The next sheet had the same stamp at the top and more numbers, but with a later date. She read the text.

Once the spores have been populated with the virus, they will be released in a small rural center by military aircraft. Twenty-four hours after the release, a research team will be inserted to test the virus's effectiveness. If the test subjects are sufficiently compliant, further tests will be conducted in a larger area.

If the second test is successful, further plans will be made to introduce the spores in all areas of the United States.

Jen swallowed. "Sufficiently compliant"?

She glanced at the signature at the bottom of the document. *Linda L. Cartwright.*

The lab door opened and Jen spun, hiding the documents with her body. Cartwright walked in. "All done with your blood?"

Jen nodded.

"Let's get you set up with accommodations," Cartwright said. "You'll be staying here in the building. Don't want your yellow eye accidentally exposed."

Cartwright put out her arm and Jen walked to the door, her pulse quickening. *How the hell am I going to get back and hide those papers? And put the cabinet back?*

As she reached Cartwright, the doctor peered past her to the desktop. "What is that?"

Cartwright walked to the desk.

25

Jen froze as Cartwright picked up the papers and studied them. Jen thought of running.

That's not an option. Just play the cards you're dealt.

"Is it true?"

Cartwright dropped the papers on the desktop and turned toward Jen. Her stern expression had softened. "I didn't want you dragged into this."

Jen crossed her arms. "Did Doc know?"

A horrified look crossed Cartwright's face. "Never. Like you, he was better off not knowing."

"So the plan was to create a mycovirus that would attach to spores and infect everyone?" Jen asked. "How were you going to keep from infecting yourself?"

Cartwright leaned on the desk, her hands at her sides grasping the edge of the desktop. "We planned on harvesting the spores from Alaska and modifying them to be short lived. Unfortunately, Mother Nature beat us to it."

"What about Butler and Morgan? Butler wasn't planning on taking down the government just so he could run it, was he?"

"No," Cartwright said. "When he found out Project Svengali would be used to control the civilian population and not just enemy forces, he played it straight, but watched and waited for the right opportunity. Morgan fled, and we spent plenty of resources trying to find him. We had no chance, though."

"Why not?"

"Colonel Butler was in charge of the search," Cartwright said. "I have no idea if he knew of Morgan's escape ahead of time, or if he found him and they decided to work together."

Jen approached Cartwright. "But, why? Why control people? Does the president just want to be a dictator?"

Cartwright took a deep breath and exhaled. "You need to believe me. It's nothing like that. We just see that the human race is an unhappy, warring people. Imagine if all decision-making was taken from you. How you'd be happy with fewer of the unnecessary gadgets and toys this world offers."

The zombies outside the door went into a frenzy. "Someone's coming," Jen said.

"I called them," Cartwright said. "Panic button underneath the desktop."

Two burly security guards strode in. Cartwright pointed at Jen. "Detain her."

Jen reached for her axe and her hand slapped an empty sheath. *Shit.*

One guard grabbed her upper arm and she twisted away.

"Don't hurt her," Cartwright said.

The two guards came at her at the same time. Jen kicked one, missing his nuts and hitting his inner thigh.

The other guard tackled her to the floor.

She squirmed. "No."

He held her down while the other guard handcuffed her. "No," she screamed.

"Pick her up."

Both guards grabbed one of Jen's arms and lifted her to her feet. She stomped on the first foot she saw. Nothing happened. *Freaking steel toe boots.*

"Shh," Cartwright said. "You're all we have."

"To defeat the zombies or to turn everyone into slaves?" Jen spat.

Cartwright shrugged. "Why not both?"

Cartwright left the lab and the guards dragged Jen kicking and screaming after her. The doctor went to an empty cell and held the door open. "In here."

"Are you fucking kidding me?" Jen grasped the bars as the straight-faced guards tried to force her in. One of them peeled her fingers off one by one. She roared as each finger was pulled back. Her teeth gritted, she lost her grip and they shoved her inside. She fell to her knees and scrambled to her feet. The door clanked shut and she rammed it, but they already had it padlocked.

"Don't do this," she yelled, grabbing bars on the door and rattling it. "Zeke and Wayne will free me."

Cartwright stood back, her arms crossed. "Your friends won't be coming back from their mission. There will be an incident on board the train on the return."

A guard handed Cartwright the key to the lock. Jen glared at her. "Doc would be so ashamed of you."

Cartwright pursed her lips then turned and left, followed by the guards.

Jen bowed her head, pressing it against the bars. *I won't cry.*

She took a deep breath and exhaled. "I've never felt so alone," she murmured.

26

Jen looked at the zombie in the next cage. A middle-aged woman with bright red hair, she had no physical damage except a bloody stump where her left pinky finger should have been. The zombie stared at Jen with her mouth hanging open. "I'll bet those yellow eyes were once a deep blue," Jen said.

She plopped herself on the bed in the corner of her cell. "Fucking great. No Zeke, no Wayne, and no D-Day."

The zombies stayed as still as statues, each gaping at her.

"So is Butler looking at me through you? Butler, you in there? Raise your right hand for yes."

The zombies didn't move.

Jen got up and paced. "You've only communicated through leaders, so maybe you can't with drones." The zombies' eyes followed her movements.

She stopped and turned toward them. "Or maybe you can hear me, like a radio transmission instead of a phone." She approached the bars separating her from the redhead and peered into the zombie's eyes. "If you can hear me, Butler, I now know what went down. How you tried to save the country." She shrugged. "Maybe that's what you're still doing."

The zombie's gaze didn't change.

Jen sighed. "I don't know what I am now, and neither does Cartwright, but she won't have any qualms about cutting me open to find out." Jen threw herself at her cell door and yanked on it furiously. "I need to get the fuck out of here."

Panting, she leaned against the door. The zombies hadn't moved. "Now you're annoying me. Why don't you all just sit down?"

As one, they dropped to the floor in a sitting position.

Jen's pulse picked up. She pointed to the redhead. "Stand up."

The redhead rose and stared at her stupidly. The other zombies remained seated.

Jen smiled. "Eight zombies. That's like having a squad at my command."

She licked her lips. "I have my way out of the building. Now I just need a way out of this cell. And I think I know how."

27

Randy carried a tray of food to her cell two hours later. The guard took off the padlock and stood to the side with a wooden baton in his beefy hand.

Jen rose from the bed as Randy stepped in and the guard shut the door.

"Hungry?" he asked.

Jen glared at him. "Really? That's what you ask? Hungry?"

Randy swallowed and turned to the guard. "Lock it up and give me five minutes."

The guard frowned.

"It's OK," Randy said. "It's part of an observation Dr. Cartwright has approved."

The guard slapped the padlock on the door and clicked it shut. "I'll be in the lab if you need me. Five minutes."

The door to the lab clicked shut behind him.

"Observation?" Jen asked.

Randy shrugged. "I had to come up with something. Can't believe it worked."

"You must think I'm not a danger," Jen said.

"I know you're not a danger," Randy said. "Cartwright probably sent me because she didn't think you'd attack me."

"She doesn't know me very well."

"Even if you do," Randy said, "I'm expendable."

He gestured to the bed. "Why don't you sit down and eat?"

Jen's stomach rumbled as he took the cover off the plate and the aroma of fried chicken enveloped her. She sat on the bed and took the tray from Randy, balancing it on her lap.

She picked up a leg and bit into it, the hot juices spilling down the sides of her mouth. In seconds, she finished the leg and dug into the mashed potatoes with a spoon.

Randy watched her. "The guard won't be gone long."

Jen squinted. "So what?"

"I want to help you."

"Because you owe me?"

"Something like that."

Jen put down the spoon. "Then have your head of physical security, Mark Colton, come see me."

Randy shook his head. "He won't come. Cartwright told him you were bitten and turned. She convinced him that he wouldn't want to see you this way."

"Then call Zeke and Wayne and let them know that Cartwright threatened to kill them. Have the decency to do at least that."

"She said she'll kill them?"

"Right to my face. They have two agents with them. My guess is those agents are the ones who'll do it. Tell them to get away as fast as possible."

Randy pushed a button on his phone. "They're in my directory. I'll call them as soon as I'm alone."

"And you'll let them know I'm here."

Randy nodded.

Jen downed a glass of water. "Why are you helping? I know you think you owe me, but aren't you on team Svengali?"

Randy shook his head. "I'd heard the name before, but had no idea what it was about until this morning." He crossed his arms and his eyes teared up. "All this bullshit. All those people dead. My mom and dad. My little brother. All because these assholes wanted to be in control." His hands clenched into fists. "No, I'm not on the fucking team." He glanced at the lab door. "But I'm letting them believe I am."

Jen put the glass down. "So why not just leave?"

"I may not know everything about Svengali and what's happened, but I do know one thing: you're the key to stopping this before we're all wiped out."

The lab door opened and the guard lumbered out. "Time's up."

Randy wiped his eyes with his shirtsleeve and gave Jen a slight nod. "I'll be back for the dishes. Take your time."

He stepped to the door. The guard looked at him.

"What?" he said.

"Strip."

"What?"

"We need to make sure she didn't bite you."

Jen nearly choked on the corn on the cob. She took a gulp of water. "You guys know I'm not a zombie, right?"

"Doctor said there's no proof your bite won't infect someone," the guard said.

I never thought of that. Could I bite someone and turn them into something like me? She turned away from Randy. "Go ahead. I won't peek."

She concentrated on her food while considering the

possibilities. *What if my bite turned people into zombies? If they found that out, then I'd never get out of here. And if it turns them into a hybrid, Cartwright will want to milk that. Crazy bitch would create an army of them.*

The cell door shut. Jen turned.

"I'll bring you breakfast in the morning," Randy said. He walked off with the guard trailing him.

Jen looked at the zombie in the next cell staring at her. "What do you think, Red? Can I trust Randy?"

Red stared.

Jen sighed. "Never thought I'd say this, but I miss Zeke's rambling stories."

JEN SAT up and rubbed her eyes. "What the hell time is it?"

Rising, she scanned the room. The zombies were still prone in their beds where she'd told them to go. *Should've told them to close their eyes, too. They'd look less creepy.*

"Red," she said, "stand up and keep me company."

Red rose, slack-jawed, and faced Jen.

Jen laughed. "My bestie is a flesh-eating corpse."

The hallway door opened and Randy entered, followed by a different guard.

"About time," Jen said. "I ordered room service an hour ago."

Randy carried a tray into the cell and the guard locked him in. Jen sat on the bed and lifted the plate cover. "Bacon and eggs." She licked her lips. Just the smell made her less hungry.

Randy stood, his hands going into his pockets, then back out and clasped in front of him.

"What are you so nervous about?" Jen said with a mouthful of eggs. "Told you I don't bite."

"Once you've eaten, I need to get a sample," he said.

Jen laughed. "Don't give me one of those little cups. I've been sitting here overnight with no bathroom."

Randy removed blood collection supplies from his pocket. "Blood sample." He looked at Red, and then at the other zombies still in bed.

"What are they doing?"

Jen downed a glass of orange juice and let out an *ahh*. "Don't know. Maybe they're tired."

She stood and walked to the cell door. "How about a bathroom break? I'm about to burst."

The guard grunted and removed the padlock. With a baton ready to strike, he pulled the door open. "In the lab. Nice and slow."

Jen took her time walking to the lab. *What would Randy do if I could take this guy out?*

She entered the lab with the guard a few steps behind. The door closed behind him. "Bathroom's in the back."

Jen's eyes scanned the room. *Need something. A weapon. A diversion. Something.*

She shuffled into the bathroom and closed the door. The guard's foot stopped it. "It'll stay open."

"Bullshit, you creep. You get off on seeing the zombie girl pee?"

The guard's face reddened. "It'll stay open two feet wide. I won't see you, but you also won't be able to pull any funny stuff."

Jen sighed. *No help in here.*

Minutes later, she approached the cell door. Randy stood inside, his arms crossed. "Ready for the sample?"

The guard pressed closer behind Jen.

Oh, shit. I've got it.

She glanced at the zombies. *Blink your eyes.*

The zombies blinked their eyes.

Yes!

She stepped around the cell door, leaving the guard on the other side.

As loud and as fast as you can, attack the guard.

The eight zombies sprang to the bars with a roar, pulling and reaching for the guard. His eyes went wide and he took a step back, ready to defend himself.

Jen grabbed the cell door and slammed it into the guard, striking him on the chest and jaw. He stumbled backward, dropping the baton and covering his broken jaw with his hands.

Scooping up his baton, Jen charged him. He reached out for her, but she ducked and raked the baton across his kneecaps. The guard howled and collapsed. Jed swung the baton and clipped his forehead, knocking the back of his head into the concrete floor. He lay still.

Jen scrambled to her feet, ready for an attack from Randy, but he hadn't moved.

The growling and clambering continued. "Stop," Jen said. "Everyone quiet."

The zombies went still, their empty yellow eyes gazing at her.

Randy's jaw dropped. "Holy shit. They listen to you?"

Jen knelt next to the guard and checked his pulse. Still alive. *Good.* She rustled through his pocket and pulled out a ring of keys. "Did you make the call to Wayne and Zeke?"

Randy nodded. "I talked to Wayne. He said they were still in Boston and it would be easy to slip away. Said they'd be gone within the hour."

"Thanks, Randy."

"No problem. He also said they'll be coming to get you."

Jen chuckled. "They know me. I'm not the damsel in distress type that's going to wait to be rescued."

Randy smiled. "That I've figured out."

She went to Red's door and tried three keys before she found the one that opened her padlock. Before opening the doors, she made eye contact with each of the zombies. She pointed at Randy. "He's off-limits. Do not harm him."

Randy pulled his cell door closed. "Not that I don't trust you."

Jen let Red out and she shambled to a position behind Jen. Within minutes, Jen had all eight zombies freed. *I could just escape, but then Cartwright would come after me. Need to keep that from happening.*

"Hand me your security badge," Jen said.

Randy unclipped it from his belt and stuck it through the bars. "What are you going to do?"

Jen squinted her eyes. "Time to pay Cartwright a little visit."

28

The elevator doors opened on the second floor. Jen pointed at two zombies, an older woman with a shredded chest and a twenty-something man with the skin peeled from one side of his skull.

"Chase anyone you see," she said. "You harm no one. Just keep running and causing chaos."

The zombies dashed out of the elevator and down the hallway. A chorus of shrieks reached Jen as the doors closed.

When they opened on the third floor, Jen picked out two more zombies. She pointed to the left. "The Security Office is just down there. Take it over. Break every piece of equipment in the place. Go."

The zombies raced from the elevator and the doors closed.

After having sent zombies out on the fourth floor, Jen was left with two: Red and a muscular bearded man with a chunk of meat missing from his shoulder.

She pressed the button for Cartwright's floor. "You two will follow me."

The doors slid open and Jen stepped out. Soft music

played from the speakers and she strode down the carpeted hallway to Cartwright's reception area. Cindy sat behind her desk and looked up as Jen walked in. "What are you—" The zombies appeared behind Jen. Cindy wrenched a drawer open and pulled a pistol.

Jen ducked. "Get out of here."

Cindy's shot took the top of the muscle man's head off and he dropped to the floor. She took aim at Red, but the zombie disappeared into the hallway.

Clenching the baton, Jen rushed Cindy and drove her to the floor, knocking the pistol from her hand. Jen wrenched Cindy's arm behind her and pulled her to her feet. Pushing Cindy toward Cartwright's office door, Jen said, "Open it."

The door opened into an empty office. "Damn," Jen said.

She pushed Cindy into a chair. "Move and I'll kill you."

She strode into the reception area and picked up Cindy's gun from underneath her desk before returning to Cartwright's office. "Where is she?"

"I don't know," Cindy said.

Jen aimed the gun at Cindy. "You're her assistant. You know, all right. Where is that bitch?"

Cindy returned Jen's glare, but said nothing.

"The bitch is right behind you," Cartwright said.

Jen spun and Cartwright stood in the doorway with a revolver pointed at her.

Jen lowered her gun. "Still looking for your ruby slippers?"

Cartwright gestured to Cindy. "Come with me. This facility is compromised. The outbreak is spreading rapidly."

Cindy walked over to Cartwright. "Where are we going?"

"To the roof. I have a helicopter coming."

"I thought they were all in the west," Jen said.

Cartwright shrugged. "Executive privilege. The president kept one for emergencies and he's sending it here."

"Are we taking her?" Cindy asked.

"Definitely," Cartwright said.

Jen jutted out her jaw. "I'm not going with a whacko like you."

"Whacko?" Cartwright said. "Is it insane to want peace and order in the world?"

Jen spat on the floor in front of Cartwright. "By taking away everyone's free will? You bet your ass it's insane."

"No matter," Cartwright said. "It's inevitable, and you're going to help make it happen quicker."

"Like hell."

Cartwright cocked the revolver's hammer back. "I'd rather you're alive for my studies, but undead should work as well."

Red sprinted into the room, colliding with Cindy and slamming her into the wall. Jen raised her gun and shot at Cartwright in one motion. A piece of doorway trim splintered and Cartwright ducked into the hallway.

A high-pitched screech pierced Jen's eardrums. Red clamped onto Cindy's neck and tore her throat out. The scream broke into a gurgle as Cindy slumped to the floor.

"No time for a snack," Jen said. "If we don't stop Cartwright now, we may not have another chance."

She raced out the door.

29

Jen raced into the corridor. Gunshots and shouting echoed from both ends. A flash of movement caught her eye. The stairway door slammed shut. Jen ran to it with Red on her heels. Several fresh zombies rushed past them, one of them leaping onto a fleeing technician. He hit the floor, his blood soaking into the carpet as the zombie tore at his back.

Innocent people are dying. What the hell have I done?

Jen flung the stairway door open and caught a glimpse of movement above. Cartwright had a head start.

Taking the steps two at a time, they reached the next floor just as the door opened and a flood of humans rushed in, knocking her and Red down. Zombies poured in after the humans, chasing them down the stairs.

Jen rubbed the back of her head where it had banged into the wall. *Got to get Cartwright.*

A zombie streaked up the stairs and stopped in front of her.

Cindy.

All undead but Red and Cindy, stand down. Do not attack anyone.

Jen struggled to her feet and stared into Cindy's yellow eyes. "I don't know if that worked or not, but it's the best I can do."

Cindy stared back.

"Take us to the roof to find Cartwright, but don't get too far ahead of us."

Cindy ran up the stairs.

Jen gestured to Red. "Let's go."

Breathing heavy, she ran up the stairs, keeping Cindy in sight. More refugees passed them going down the stairs, but Cindy and Red ignored them as they followed Jen's directions.

Cindy waited at the top of the stairway. Jen caught up with her and bent over with her hands on her knees. Her chest heaved and her heart slammed her chest. "Top floor," she gasped.

Jen pushed the door open and stepped into a quiet tiled hallway. A corridor stretched ahead and another to the right.

Jen held the door open. "Get in."

The two zombies lumbered in and stopped.

Jen listened. "It's like the outbreak hasn't hit here yet."

A gunshot echoed down the corridor and a piece of the doorframe behind Jen exploded. Jen ducked.

An armed guard knelt in a room at the end of the hallway with a pistol propped against the door frame. He shot again, and the bullet buried into Cindy's shoulder.

Jen took cover around the corner. "With me."

The zombies followed.

Sticking her gun out, Jen fired off three blind rounds. The guard answered in kind.

"Who's betting Cartwright went that way?" she said. She peered farther down the corridor they hid in. "I wonder if there's a back way."

Footsteps came from the direction of the guard. Jen popped her head out and back in. A barrage of gunshots replied. Three more guards had made their way halfway down the corridor and another stayed back providing supporting fire. *Where the hell did those other guys come from?*

She fired two more blind rounds then peeked around the corner. The guards returned fire and Jen barely pulled her head back in time. *They're holding position. Too far away for us to rush them. But if I can get one of them on our side...*

"Girls, when I tell you, I want you to run out into view, pause, then run back here."

Jen ejected the pistol's magazine and checked the load. *Five rounds. With one in the chamber, that's not much.* She slapped the magazine back in. "Got to make them count."

She moved as close to the corner as she could without being seen and turned to face the wall so when she stepped out into the hall she would face them. Squatting, she held the pistol in two hands and took a deep breath. *Don't rush.*

"Now, girls. Go."

The zombies ran past her and Jen leaned to the left and stretched out, landing on her side.

Bullets flew by and some hit solid wood and some smacked into undead flesh.

Take your time.

Lining up the sights on one of the three guards, she took a deep breath, then let half of it out. She squeezed the trigger.

The bullet hit the guard in the throat. He clutched his neck and fell over.

Jen was already aiming at the guard at the end of the corridor.

A bullet chipped the tile next to her, shrapnel cutting her cheek. She ignored the sting. *Girls, do the same thing again.*

The guns that were aimed at her swung toward the zombies as they exposed themselves to gunfire again. Jen concentrated on her target. With only half his body in the open, her aim had to be true.

Just as she squeezed the trigger, the first guard she shot rose, snarling, his yellow eyes gleaming. He attacked his two companions from the rear.

The pistol recoiled and Jen's target at the end of the corridor dropped his gun and grabbed his shoulder. She sent a follow-up shot, but missed as he rolled out of sight.

"Attack, girls."

The two guards had turned to face the threat from behind and realized too late they were surrounded. One of them wrestled with the zombie guard while the other shot wildly at Red and Cindy. Red pounced on him and tore open his shoulder with her teeth. Cindy tackled the other guard and chewed on his arm while the zombie guard went for his throat.

"Everyone to me."

The three zombies shuffled to Jen's side. *I wonder how many I can control at once? Butler can do millions, but he goes through his leaders.*

As she crept down the corridor to the open doorway, the other two guards rose. "Fall in with the others," Jen said.

She paused at the doorway and peeked inside. It was a large stock room with cabinets, a sink, and cleaning equipment. A trail of blood ran from the doorway to thick metal stairs that led to an upper level.

Can't see the whole thing. Someone could be up there.

Keeping her pistol pointed upward, she dashed to the stairs and pointed at one of the guards. "You first. Go quickly."

The zombie raced up the stairs and Jen followed.

The upper level was bare except for another stairway with a sign next to it that read "Roof Access."

"Could be a nice place for an ambush." Jen chewed her lip. "Go to be careful. I don't know how many guns she has up there."

A distant muffled sound caught her ear. *Sounds familiar.*

The sound came closer. *Thup thup thup.*

Time's up.

30

Jen sprinted up the stairs. "Let's go."

A guard stood in front of the roof door, his pistol aimed at her. Jen swung her barrel toward him and stopped.

"Mark?"

"Stop there, Jen," Mark said.

Red stepped next to Jen as the other zombies crowded her from behind on the stairs. Mark's eyebrows rose.

"Cartwright was right," he said.

"Right about what?" Jen said. "What'd she tell you?"

"That you're not the Jen I know and love. That you're...different."

Jen sighed. "Some things are different, but I'm still the same person who fought all those battles at your side."

Mark shook his head. "That Jen never had her own zombie army."

"OK, smart-ass. That part's different, but it's still me."

Mark looked from Jen to the zombies and back. "Why would she tell me that if it isn't true?"

Jen tilted her head and listened. The helicopter had to be just overhead. "Because she's been lying to us since the beginning. She's the cause of this shit. She and her co-conspirators have been working on a way to control people."

"Put the gun down," Mark said. "I don't want to shoot you."

Jen jerked a thumb over her shoulder. "You do and I won't be able to save you from them."

Mark remained silent. *He's processing what tactical advantages and disadvantages he has.*

Jen took a step toward him he pointed the gun from her chest to her head. "Stop."

"Shoot me in the head?"

"Least I can do for who you were."

Jen gritted her teeth. "Look, asshole, I'm still me, and you're wasting time. Cartwright's going to get away."

Mark's eyes narrowed.

"Just step aside and get out of here," Jen said. "Get your family out and far away."

Another sound outside. Something hitting the roof? *The helicopter has landed. Out of time.*

"How can I prove to you I'm still me?"

Mark shrugged.

"How about that I haven't sicced these guys on you?" she asked.

Mark paused, then said, "You know I'll shoot you first, so you won't take the chance."

Dammit, you stubborn ass.

Precious seconds ticked away. Faces and events with Mark flashed through her mind. When they first met in her room. Talking on the roof and finding out his pain. Her saving his ass. Him saving hers. Zeke. Doc. *Doc.*

That's it.

Jen straightened. "Mark, if I'm not telling you the truth, I'll eat a bug."

Mark's expression remained unchanged, then his shoulders relaxed a little. He gazed into her eyes. "Jen?"

"It's me. A little fucked up, but you know me well enough to know that's a normal state for me."

Mark licked his lips, then straightened and lowered his gun.

Jen pointed at him. "Not only are you not to harm him or his family, but you will protect him from others. Human and zombie."

"Will that really work?" Mark asked.

"Who the hell knows? Move aside."

Mark stepped to the side.

Jen gave him a quick hug. "Promise me you'll get your family and get out of here."

"I promise. But I should help you get Cartwright first."

"I've got all the troops I need, and your mother and sister need you right now."

She turned to the zombies. "Follow me and attack anyone on the roof. Except Red and Cindy. You two stay with me."

Bulling the door open, she rushed onto the roof. Gunfire came from the Blackhawk that had landed on the far end of the roof. Cartwright was just boarding. Three guards next to the helicopter opened fire on the charging zombies.

No time for tactics. Jen broke into a full run toward the helicopter. *If I can get close enough to at least take a good shot at Cartwright...*

The helicopter lifted a couple of inches. One of the guards looked back at it and yelled. He and the others made a run for it, but were brought down by their fellow guards from behind.

The helicopter moved a few feet up and away from the roof. Jen's gaze locked on Cartwright's. For the first time, the bitch smiled.

Heat flared in Jen's face. "Cindy. Jump on the helicopter."

Cindy sprinted past Jen, making a beeline for the helicopter. Cartwright pointed at her and said something. The helicopter started ascending just as Cindy leapt. She missed the door and wrapped her arms on a landing skid.

Guards, follow Cindy. Get your weight on that helicopter.

The guards left their meal and streaked toward the helicopter. Cartwright gestured frantically and looked like she was screaming into her headset. The pilot gritted his teeth and the helicopter began to rise again.

The guards leapt. The first one missed and dropped out of sight, but the next three hit with two of them managing to hang on.

The helicopter descended. The pilot screamed into his mic and flipped several switches.

Jen slowed. "Red, I need you to take out the tail rotor."

Red shot past Jen and leapt at the rotor. She hit it and turned into a pink mist.

"Shit. That did nothing?"

The helicopter pulled away, the zombies still clinging to the skids. It barely made it over nearby buildings and it moved slow, but it was moving.

"Son of a bitch. She's going to get away."

The *thup thup thup* of the rotors changed rhythm and Jen shaded her eyes to get a better look. The tail rotor seemed to be slowing. As she watched, it stopped altogether.

"You did it, Red."

The helicopter started spinning, black smoke trailing

from the rear. One by one, the zombies clinging to the skids were thrown off.

Losing altitude, the helicopter dropped out of sight somewhere near Emory University. Seconds later a thick plume of black smoke rose into the air.

31

Jen adjusted her sunglasses as she walked toward the helicopter wreckage. Two students stood next to the blackened skeleton and looked up as she approached.

"Hell of a thing," one student, a beefy jock-looking kid said. "Everyone thought all the aircraft went west, but they say the CDC kept one for emergencies." He kicked a burned piece of metal. "Shame they wrecked the damn thing."

The skinny long-haired girl next to him pushed one brown lock behind her ear. "I heard the military is pissed about it."

"Anyone survive?" Jen asked.

The boy shrugged, but the girl nodded. "I heard four died and one survived. At least long enough to go to the hospital. Good thing it's close by, the bodies were supposedly pretty burned up."

I heard. I think. Can't get a straight answer anymore. "Could you point me to Clifton Road?"

The boy pointed at a large building looming over the trees. "Just the other side of the hospital."

Jen hiked up her backpack. "Thanks."

Walking up to the brick-faced house on Ridgeway Drive, Jen had an uneasy feeling in her gut. *Looks more like a typical suburban family lives here, not some bikers.*

She took the walk to the front door and rang the doorbell, fully prepared to tell the homeowner she had the wrong house. When no one answered, she shaded her eyes and peered through the window.

Inside looked just as nice as the outside. It had the kind of furniture she wouldn't dare sit on in case it broke.

An engine roared to life from somewhere behind the house. She crossed the perfectly manicured grass to the driveway that wound around to the back. A standalone garage came into view with its two overhead doors open. Three men and a woman worked on three motorcycles. Even among his own people, D-Day stood out, bent over and working on the sidecar.

Jen approached, and as soon as the woman shut off the engine she was gunning, Jen waved and said, "D-Day."

D-Day straightened as the others reached for weapons.

He put a hand out to the others. "She's cool."

Wiping his hands on a greasy rag, he loped to Jen. "Needing some help?"

She nodded. "A lot has happened. I'll tell you all about it on the road."

White teeth appeared under D-Day's mustache. "On the road. I like that. Where are we going?"

"West."

32

Jen wiped up egg yolk with her last piece of toast and placed it in her mouth.

"What did Wayne and Zeke say?" D-Day asked.

Washing down the food with some orange juice, Jen put up a finger. "They're in Pennsylvania. Told them we're heading for Colorado so they have a general direction."

"Did you say Colorado, young lady?" An older man in faded jeans, a cotton shirt, boots, and a cowboy hat stood next to their table.

D-Day nodded. "What's it to you?"

"I didn't mean to eavesdrop," the cowboy said, "but you're heading right into the front lines. News this morning said the undead have overrun Salt Lake City and are heading east. They expect Colorado to be the next major battleground."

Jen downed the rest of her orange juice and looked from the cowboy to D-Day. "Then Colorado it is."

CONTINUE THE JOURNEY

To keep up to date on the release of the next book in the Zombie Uprising Series, go to www.marobbins.com.

AUTHOR'S NOTES

In many ways The Hybrid is a lynchpin in the series. It answers some questions going all the way back to Book One, The Awakening, and sets the table for the rest of the series.

This was the first book of the series that was written after the The Awakening was released to the public, and reader reactions to the series gave me plenty of motivation and inspiration to keep the series moving along.

We're now heading into the fall and winter where my writing pace usually picks up. Other than a trip to Pittsburgh for Night of the Living Dead 50th anniversary events, and a follow-on to New England to see family, I'll be holed up in front of the computer, pounding away at the keyboard. Like you, I can't wait to see what happens next.

If you'd like to keep up with what I've got coming out, sign up for my email list at uprising.marobbins.com. You'll get a **free** eBook, new release announcements, updates, and even some drawings to win prizes like signed paperbacks and other unique items.

Thank you so much for reading the Hybrid. Know that I

take no reader for granted and I'm truly humbled that you spent your time reading my book.

Till next time.

M.A. Robbins

ACKNOWLEDGMENTS

Thanks go to my wife, Debbie, for her steadfast support. Tamara Blain, editor extraordinaire at A Closer Look Editing, was a godsend for this book as events gave her a shorter turnaround time and she aced it with a smile. Domi at Inspired Cover Designs just keeps adding to her legend. To the beta readers, I really appreciate your input and honesty. You made the book better.

To all the readers, I've received such positive feedback since the series launched in May 2018. Rest assured that I'm putting my heart and soul into the books to provide you with top-notch zombie action. Thank you for reading!

ALSO BY M.A. ROBBINS

The Zombie Uprising Series
    The Awakening, Book One
    The Gauntlet, Book Two
    The Citadel, Book Three

The Tilt Series
    The Tilt, Book One

Printed in Great Britain
by Amazon